Guardian

"A pitch-perfect blend of humour, adventure and emotion"
Sunday Telegraph

"Funny, entertaining and surprisingly moving and it is this …
that lifts the book above the ordinary"
Philip Ardagh, *Guardian*

"*Sparks* has a beautiful emotional intelligence and humour that
make its suspense all the more enjoyable. It is one of the best
new books for 9+ out this year"
The Times

"Enterprising writing of a high calibre"
Independent on Sunday

"Proof that magic is really all around us"
Guardian

"Ally Kennen began her writing career well with an acclaimed book
for teens and has gone from strength to strength with each
subsequent novel… Well-observed, witty and moving"
Sunday Times

"Ally Kennen is a wonderful storyteller and she draws the reader in
to this novel with its excellent characterisation and bittersweet plot"
Scotsman

"Inventive, funny and moving family adventure ...
one of the season's stand-outs"
Children's Bookseller – Ones to Watch

"Refreshingly different ... a well written tale with much wisdom
embedded in the telling. Words that are inspiring, challenging
and encouraging convey the message that the beloved dead
are always with us to inspire, challenge, encourage"
School Librarian

"Rings with talent and compelling detail ...
a tense, funny and touching tale"
Amanda Craig, *The Times*

"Ally Kennen is already a remarkably assured writer"
Nicholas Tucker, *Independent*

"An extraordinary imaginative achievement ... this is a compassionate
story from an exciting new voice"
Bookseller

ALLY KENNEN grew up on a farm in Exmoor. She is the author of eight novels for children and teens. Her books have been nominated for and won numerous awards.

She lives in Somerset with her husband, three children, chickens, a dog and four and a half cats.

Her ambitions are to write many more books and join a women's football team.

allykennen.blogspot.com

Also by Ally Kennen

MIDNIGHT PIRATES
SPARKS

Young Adult Titles

BEAST
BEDLAM
BERSERK
QUARRY
BULLET BOYS

HOW TO SPEAK SPOOK

(AND STAY ALIVE)

ALLY KENNEN

■SCHOLASTIC

Scholastic Children's Books
A division of Scholastic Ltd.
Euston House, 24 Eversholt Street
London, NW1 1DB, UK
Registered office: Westfield Road, Southam, Warwickshire, CV47 0RA
SCHOLASTIC and associated logos are trademarks and/
or registered trademarks of Scholastic Inc.

First published in the UK by Scholastic Ltd, 2015

ISBN 978 1407 14875 5
A CIP catalogue record for this book
is available from the British Library

Printed and bound by CPI Group (UK) Ltd, Croydon CR0 4YY
Papers used by Scholastic Children's Books
are made from wood grown in sustainable forests.

1 3 5 7 9 10 8 6 4 2

This is a work of fiction. Names, characters, places, incidents
and dialogues are products of the author's imagination or are used fictitiously.
Any resemblance to actual people, living or dead, events
or locales is entirely coincidental.

www.scholastic.co.uk

For Harry Kennen

CHAPTER ONE

The Extraordinary Gifts of Donald Memphis

Have you ever wished you were freakishly brilliant at something? Maybe you ARE brilliant at something. You might be the Queen of Leaking Secrets, or the King of Sleeplessness. Or maybe you are SO gifted and talented, you get awarded certificates by the headmaster at school every week, for gravity-busting work in the science lab, or Olympian feats in PE lessons.

Donald Memphis, in all his eleven years, had only once been given a certificate in assembly, and that was five years ago.

Mr Vellow, the headmaster, had read it out to the entire school.

Certificate of Achievement

Awarded to Donald Memphis for putting his shoes on fairly quickly.

Mr Vellow had fired an incredulous look at Donald's teacher, who had shrugged, as if to say, "*What could I do? I've got to give him a certificate for something and the boy is completely thick.*"

Though of course she did not say it. Nowadays teachers are not allowed to say such things no matter how much they yearn to.

Donald's friend Merry was fabulously talented. She got beamed out of lessons for extra tricky maths with other gifted children and played piano in school concerts. She had many folders of certificates from the headmaster and used the Greek alphabet to organize them.

But Donald found normal maths tricky enough, let alone tricky maths; he had trouble enough pronouncing the word "alphabet" (he said "alforget"), let alone knowing the Greek one; and the only time the headmaster had spoken to him in the last five years was when he'd stepped on Donald whilst showing the school inspectors around. And then he'd said:

"Why ON EARTH are you lying in the middle of the corridor?"

Which Donald had been unable to answer because

a)   he couldn't find the right words and
b)   the headmaster wouldn't believe him.

Because Donald was spying on a small child ghost wedged in the wall who was doing a monkey dance. But you can't go telling headmasters this kind of thing, even if you have A Way With Words, which Donald did not. His words often got lost on the long journey from his brain to his mouth, and when they left his body they were often in the wrong order, especially when he was talking to Important People.

In the end he had just said "ouch", because it hurts when headmasters step on you.

But now it was Friday and it was home time and, as Merry lived next door to Donald, they were walking home together. At Brunel Primary, boys DID NOT have girls as friends and girls NEVER had boys as friends, so Merry and Donald were NOT FRIENDS.

I'm glad that is clear.

There had just been another assembly and yet again, Donald hadn't got a certificate.

"Even Danny Olini got one," said Donald gloomily.

Danny Olini.

His certificate had looked like this:

Certificate of Achievement

Awarded to Danny Olini for not hitting anyone all week.

Danny was sort of Donald's friend, even though Donald avoided him whenever he could. Danny had concrete fists, didn't care if he got told off, and had a habit of climbing out of classroom windows.

He was the kind of boy who, if he was mentioned in a book, would get a line to himself.

CHAPTER ONE

The girl with the long black hair watched as a human missile dived into the pool and fished the drowning witch from the bottom.

Danny Olini.

"Where do witches make cakes?" he called. He liked the girl and wanted to make her laugh.

"In their covens. Get it? C. Ovens."

The girl did not laugh.

See?

Danny had a bit of carpet by the paint cupboard which was his "Safe Space". Though Donald called it his "Space Safe". Whenever Danny sat on his Safe Space, Donald imagined him surrounded by stars and moons. No wonder it calmed him down.

"You don't need certificates to show you are special," said Merry. "You're the most talented person I know." For despite being extraordinarily talented, Merry was kind, even to people who WERE NOT her friends. She was small with dark eyes and a thick black plait. She wore boys' school shorts over girls' tights and a red coat to keep out the February chill. Donald, by contrast, was a solid sort of person, with light brown hair and the sort of face that goes reddy-pink very quickly. Right now he had a toothpaste crust smeared on his lower lip which must have been there all day. Offering him a mint, Merry decided it was not worth mentioning.

No, Donald was not top of the class. He had something much better than that.

He had The Gift.

The gift of second sight.

Donald could see and hear ghosts.

He also had the gift of third sight.

Because they could see and hear him.

He also had the gift of fourth sight.

He could chat to them.

And he had the gift of fifth, or foresight.

He could sometimes tell what was going to happen.

And he had the gift of sixth, or hindsight.

He could tell what had happened in the past (this isn't special; everyone has this).

And Donald Memphis had the gift of seventh sight.

He could sometimes tell what people were thinking.

And he had the gift of eighth sight. . . All right, you get the idea.

Donald could do other things. He could taste Mondays (peanuts) and he knew that danger was a pure, brilliant white. He knew the word "amble" rustled like a bag of crisps.

Most of this he kept to himself, because he guessed, correctly, that people would find it all too strange. Merry didn't find it strange because she could sometimes see ghosts too, only a billion times less than Donald.

"I wish I could do something Normally Brilliant," said Donald wistfully. "Something that would impress teachers."

He'd had a tough day, having lost his new PE trainers, failed to finish his English essay, accidentally flattened tiny Daisy Lockett in the playground, and expelled a small but lively fart right next to his teacher. Mrs Hutchins had told him to "pull himself together", and other things he didn't like to remember. Then she'd put her head out of the window and taken a Deep Breath.

Mrs Hutchins only put her head out of the window and took Deep Breaths when she needed to calm down. She said it was because she needed air, but the children knew it was Mrs Hutchins's own Safe Space, just like Danny Olini's.

At the corner of the street, where the road forked, Donald stopped.

"I'm going to see my dad," he told Merry.

"Can I come?"

Donald thought. "Better not. He gets nervous with people."

"That's ironic," said Merry.

Donald nodded sagely, though he had no idea what "ironic" meant. Something to do with ironing? Or was it more like a cousin of "moronic"? The word tasted tangy, like licking a 2p.

Merry beetled off home, swinging her homework-stuffed satchel in risky circles.

Donald crossed the road, hurried down a footpath and arrived in a quiet narrow street.

Something was following him. He sneaked a look over his shoulder.

Nothing was following him.

He stood in front of a tall, orangey house. The paint was peeling from the walls and some of the roof tiles were gone. The building had boarded-up windows and the garden was thick with nettle skeletons and wintery-dead plants. Nothing about the house indicated that anyone lived there.

This was Larry Memphis's house. Donald's dad, though he didn't *live* there either, not exactly.

Let me explain.

When Donald was very young, he discovered three important facts about his family.

1) His parents had split up.
2) Dad was dead.
3) Despite the other facts, Dad still wanted to see Donald.
   And when Donald was a bit bigger, he realized one more important fact.
4) Dad was actually a ghost.

(Yes, yes, you read that bit right. At least I hope you did. If you read "4) Dad saw an exploding rabbit" then you read it wrong. Go back and read number 4 again or you will MISS the WHOLE point of the story.)

The front gate was padlocked shut. Donald prodded

in the combination code, stepped over chalky-dry cat poo and hurried up the path to the house before anyone saw him. This was the house Dad had moved into after he and Donald's mum had split up.

Donald fitted his key into the lock and the door opened with a drawn-out creak.

The hallway was dark. Dust had settled on every surface and the air smelled like old eggshells. As Donald walked, the air temperature plummeted. He pushed open a green door at the end and stepped through.

"Dad?"

CHAPTER TWO

Ghost Dad

The room was dazzling. Mirrors of every size hung from the walls. Spinning window crystals sent rainbows racing over Donald's face and a silver glitter ball shot out flashing bullets of light. Tall shelves, packed tight with records, dominated one wall, and a large record player sat importantly on a low table.

You don't know what records are? They are black discs of music made of vinyl, a kind of hard plastic.

They had them in the olden days, when no one wore seat belts or brushed their teeth in the mornings.

If you find one, don't eat it.

A long white sofa covered with yellow shiny cushions sat

under the window and a polished guitar rested against the mirrored wall.

A record revolved silently round the turntable.

Donald kept his coat on because it was as cold inside as it was out. Ghosts don't need central heating.

"Dad?"

Donald knew ghosts faded and faded, until they eventually vanished altogether. The idea filled him with dread. He studied the wide, gilt-edged mirror over the fireplace. Sometimes Dad appeared there first. But today Donald saw nothing but reflections of reflections of himself.

Donald shut his eyes. This was an old trick. If he opened them quickly, he often caught sight of a something, slipping into the space between then and now.

"Dad, I've lost my trainers, and Mum will eliminate me like a slug if I don't find them," gabbled Donald.

"Under the sofa."

A figure stood by the door.

"Hello, son."

Larry Memphis had died in mysterious circumstances when he was thirty-seven years old. His ghost had a sprinkle of beard and short dark hair. He always wore the same black-and-white rugby top and loose grey jeans. As his face came into focus, it broke into a wide grin. His eyes twinkled as a shard of light passed over him.

"You've got to listen to this record, darling," said Dad, in his deep friendly voice. He crossed the room and picked an album from a section of the shelves marked *Z*.

"It's by a band called Led Zeppelin, and this tune is

called 'Stairway to Heaven'. It's the song you must learn on guitar if you want to impress girls."

"Dad, I'm eleven years old. I spend my time trying to annoy girls, not impress them," said Donald, trying not to show how worried he had been about the fading business. "And don't call me darling. It's embarrassing."

"What about Merry?" asked Dad, hugging his son. The amazing, incredible thing about Dad was, despite being dead, he could hug and be hugged. Dad felt solid and THERE, even though he technically wasn't.

"Merry's not a girl," said Donald swiftly. "She's a human."

Dad laughed and held out the record. "Can you put it on? I'm feeling weak this morning. I might scratch it."

Donald felt a stab of concern. "Not like *fading* weak?"

"No, no, NO," Dad assured him. "Just a touch of man flu."

"Can ghosts get flu?"

"This one can."

Donald took the black disc from its paper sleeve and swapped it with the other record on the turntable. He set the needle on the rim, the disc began to turn and Dad's broad face filled with joy.

"You ought to convert all these records to digital," said Donald, turning up the volume. "Records are so old-fashioned." Donald never seemed to have any problems with words when he was with his dad. They flew out, like he'd borrowed someone else's tongue.

That is a bad thought. Let us forget it.

You haven't forgotten it, have you? No one could forget borrowing someone else's tongue. I will have to say something drastic to distract you.

WITCHES' CRUSTING NOSTRILS.

Forgotten? Good. We can move on.

"I'm dead, I don't care about being old-fashioned," chuckled Dad. "I love my records."

"Is that why you came back from the grave?" asked Donald. "To protect your record collection?"

"Partly," said Dad sheepishly. "But the main reason is to keep an eye on you."

Donald visited Dad at least two or three times a week. When Donald was little, his mother would drop him off at the front door, wait for it to slowly swing open and tell him she'd be back in an hour.

"Why don't you ever come in?" Donald asked her once.

"You'll understand when you're older," replied his mother. "But I've seen enough of that man to last a lifetime, let alone an afterlife time." For Donald's mum could see ghosts too. In fact, seeing ghosts was her job.

The music built to a crescendo and then calmed, slipping into the last clear notes. Donald nodded appreciatively.

"What did you think of that?" asked Dad, his face shining with happiness.

"Goodish," said Donald.

"I knew you'd love it," said Dad, beaming. "And luckily for you, I have seven albums' worth."

"Why do you love music so much?" Donald asked.

Dad cocked his fingers to make a steeple. "When you're

12

dead, your senses are dull. I can touch your cheek and feel warmth, sometimes I wonder if it is only my memory. But my sight and hearing are fine. Listening to good music makes me forget I'm dead."

Donald flopped on the sofa and a cloud of dust made him cough. Dad eyed him.

"What's wrong?"

Donald thought. What was wrong was that he thought his dad was finally beginning to fade. Also what was wrong was that his schoolwork seemed really really difficult at the moment and he never got any certificates. A boy needs praise! Also, he was seeing so many ghosts everywhere he was beginning to mix up the living and the dead.

"Well?"

Donald decided to go for the safest answer.

"I'm feeling stupid. I'm struggling with maths," he admitted. "When I put a number in my head, it gets swallowed up before I can do anything with it."

He trod on a light dancing over the floor.

"I'm also having trouble with my English. The letters wriggle, like tadpoles in a feeding frenzy."

"Anything else?" asked Dad gently.

"Science is confusing," said Donald, fiddling with the record sleeve. "In experiments, everyone gets different answers. So how do you know which is the right one?"

"You like French?"

"I like quiche," said Donald. "That's French, right?"

"Sounds tough. How are your friends?" Dad's face darkened. "Are you still playing with Danny Olini?"

13

"Kinda. Danny Olini plays like he's the cat and you're the mouse. He likes smacking you about for fun. But nobody picks on me when he's around."

Dad picked up the acoustic guitar and began to strum a few chords. Donald knew what was coming. Dad thought music was the answer to everything. Sure enough, he began to sing.

"Fractions mean distractions
And times tables are number fables.
Who can tell if you can't spell?"

"Stop," pleaded Donald. "I beg you."

"You can see into the afterlife!" said Dad. "That's not stupid!"

"Not much use when you can't spell 'tomorrow'," sighed Donald.

"You communicate with spirits!"

"A lot of Nothings are pretty boring," said Donald. "Except you, of course," he added hurriedly.

Butting in here, I must explain that Donald often called ghosts "Nothings". This was because when people asked him what he was looking at, he'd got in the habit of replying, "Nothing".

"Nothing" was a safer reply than "Dead Things".

"Cheer up, school won't last very long," Dad said wisely. "But you can see into eternity."

"Even though I can't tell the time," muttered Donald. "Unless it's digital."

Dad knelt on the floor and held out his palms. At once all the motes of light and rainbows which had been dancing round the room flew into his hands and ran up his arms.

"Wow," said Donald as Dad poured the stream of sparkling gold and silver into Donald's fingers. It felt like thousands of warm bubbles were bursting on his skin. He could almost hear the light; it sounded like a sweet, vibrating chord of music and tasted of vanilla.

"You're a magic boy," said Dad, watching him fondly. "You can do and see things most people can only dream of."

And after that, there were more records and even a shop-bought cheese sandwich which Dad had somehow got hold of. When it was time to go, Dad hugged him.

"Wish I could come with you."

"Mum would exorcize you," said Donald.

"Don't joke," shuddered Dad.

"Dad?"

"Yes?"

"Why aren't you still alive?"

"Because I'm dead," said Dad, looking as shifty as a ghost can when he is wearing a rugby shirt and has just listened to his favourite records with his favourite person.

"But why are you dead?" persisted Donald.

"Everyone dies," said Dad.

Donald scowled. "Why is it secret?"

Dad stood directly in front of a mirror.

"It's complicated." His right arm seemed to blend into the light.

"You're fading," snapped Donald. Dad had a habit of vanishing when asked difficult questions.

"I'll tell you one day," said Dad. "Maybe."

"But it makes me think it was something really, really bad," admitted Donald.

Dad was getting fainter. Donald could see right through him to his record collection.

"It was just unfortunate," said Dad, his voice sounding like he was a long way away.

Donald was desperate to know more. But the sun went behind a cloud, the lights and rainbows vanished and the needle of the record player slid off the disc and went silent.

Donald blinked. He was standing in an empty room.

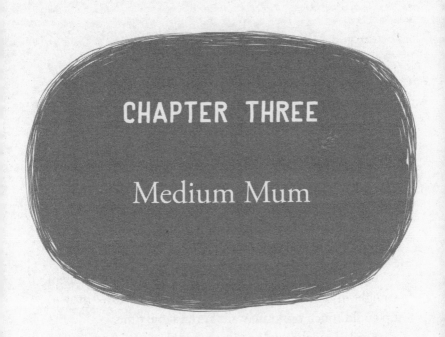

CHAPTER THREE

Medium Mum

It took Donald ages, nearly forty-five seconds, to walk from his dad's place to home. In that time he spotted the old lady ghost who waited at the corner, ghost pigeons fighting over some chips and a ghost hedgehog about to cross the road without looking.

Donald's house was unusual.

Two hundred years ago, some person (who, WHO would have done this and WHY? We will never know) had decided to build a house in the alleyway between an old vicarage (Merry's house) and a chapel.

According to Donald's mum, theirs was the third narrowest house in Great Britain. It looked like this:

Donald stepped through the door from the pavement straight into the living room, which was so narrow a grown-up could touch opposite walls at the same time.

April, Donald's mum, was sitting on the floor in the living room, rifling through a box of chipped crystal balls. She was wearing her favourite purple velvet skirt and her black sparkly top. She was a smallish woman with a round face and big eyes. Her long, shiny brown hair lay in a ponytail over her shoulder.

Merry said Mum was pretty but Donald wouldn't know. She was his mother.

"I'm getting rid of a few bits and bobs," she said, squinting at him short-sightedly. (She was too vain to wear her glasses all the time.) "This house is too small. It was built for the vicar's mother in 1816. She was getting so old and stinky the vicar didn't want her living with him any more, so he built this ridiculous house in the alleyway."

"Why are you telling me this now?" asked Donald, looking away from the crystal balls. He didn't like the things; they reminded him of eyeballs.

"I thought you'd be interested," said Mum.

Donald's mother was always getting rid of things. It was one of her favourite activities. Another favourite was shopping at jumble sales and charity shops, so she was always carting things into or out of the house.

Donald dropped his school bags on the floor and perched on the squashy black sofa that took up half the room. The other half had a fireplace, with a real fire, a bookshelf and the smallest television you ever saw in your life. Donald's mum bought it from a camping shop and it was the size of a shoebox.

"Did you like school today?" asked Mum, anxiously.

"School did not like me," replied Donald. "I saw Dad on the way home."

Mum rummaged some more. "How is he?"

"Shifty," said Donald. "He played lots of records."

Mum sniffed and tossed her ponytail over her other shoulder. "It used to drive me loopy, music playing all the time."

"Is that why you stopped being married?" asked Donald.

His mother looked up from her box. "Not now, Donald."

"Why is he dead anyway?" Donald felt there was nothing to lose by asking her again. After all, he'd only asked her three hundred billion times already.

"Not now, Donald," repeated Mum.

"It's always Not Now," grumbled Donald. "When will the Yes Now come?"

Mum sat back on her heels. "We've got a job. A serious haunting."

"You changed the subject," complained Donald.

"Yes," said Mum. "Don't try and change it back."

Mum was a Medium. Other words for Mediums are:

Clairvoyants

Mystics

Diviners

Psychics

People Who Have Extrasensory Perception (ESP)

Spiritualists

People Who Have the Second Sight

People Who Have The Gift

But Mum liked to call herself a "Ghost Liaison Officer".

If someone was having trouble with ghosts, they'd hire Mum to sort it out. Donald often went along too, to keep an eye on things.

Very often ghosts became "active" because they were annoyed about something. Mum's job was to find out:

a) If there were ghosts there.
b) What they were annoyed about (if anything).
c) What could be done to make them happy.

Mum was fond of levels and marks and points and had devised a system for marking ghost infestation levels. Nearly every house in England over ten years old was at least a level one, though no one ever worried about those. Mum was interested in anything over a level five. These hauntings usually involved spirits that wanted to communicate with the living, even if it was just chucking a few plates around. The bigger the disturbance, the higher the level.

When she wasn't dealing with ghosts, Mum had a shop, called Charms, in a narrow road just off the high street, which sold stuff like crystals and fortune-telling cards. The shop wasn't open very often because Mum wasn't very good at turning up at work, and when you are the boss (which she was) it means no one can give you the sack.

Donald's stomach rumbled. "Can I have the bun in your bag?"

"What bun?" Mum snatched her bag off the floor.

Donald held out his hand. "Pleeeeease."

"In a minute. Where are my glasses?" Mum turned over a cushion.

"You should know, you're the psychic," said Donald. Mum was always losing things.

"Aha!" She drew her glasses out of her bag, then extracted the bun.

"Eat this and then we're going out. We're late."

"But I've only just got in," said Donald, taking the bun and biting into it. The sweetness spread over his tongue and he thought of sunsets.

"One for me?" asked Mr Thomas Jones, who was a ghost, and had appeared on the kitchen step wearing his dirty boots and holding a garden fork.

More information about Mr Thomas Jones will follow shortly, but right now, there is not time.

Just WAIT.

Ghosts do not always appear at convenient moments.

"See you later, Thomas," said Mum.

Two minutes later, they were sitting in Mum's green van, which was named The Charmer.

"Where are we going?" Donald strapped himself in next to his mother.

"A place which has reported an extraordinarily high level of haunting," replied Mum, patting the dashboard fondly because The Charmer had started after only the third attempt.

As they drove through the darkening streets, Donald wondered where this place could be. Maybe it was somewhere ancient and majestic. A place of mystery and shadows, where supernatural forces battled with time itself.

Mum pulled into a supermarket car park.

"We're here."

"I know we're **here**," said Donald. "But when are we going to be **THERE**?" He hated supermarkets. They made his brain hurt.

"Where's There?" asked Mum, reversing into a space.

"'There' is where the ghosts are," said Donald.

"This is There," said Mum, opening her door with a long creak.

Donald looked in disbelief at the shining glass walls and blazing colours of the store. Everyone knows ghosts prefer quiet places.

He did his eye-face. The face he did when he did not believe what his mother was telling him.

"Don't pull your eye-face," said Mum. "Come and see."

Next to the entrance, Donald saw a boy spirit, aged about eight and dressed in breeches and a dirty grey cotton shirt, perched on top of a row of trolleys. Mum had not seen him.

"Who were you?" Donald asked the spirit.

"Jack," said Jack. "I bin dead for five hundred years. Nice dog."

"I haven't got a dog," said Donald.

"Oh," said Jack and picked at his grey teeth.

"Do you know what the problem is here?" asked Donald. From the outside, the shop looked like a normal supermarket, with glass walls, cash machines and screaming kids.

"Don't go in," said Jack. "It's proper haunted."

"But you're a ghost."

"Yeah, I got run over by the undertaker's horse out in the car park. But I wouldn't never go in there, not if you paid me one whole penny."

"Why not?" asked Donald, going in anyway.

"Too scary," said Jack.

Mum was chatting to a man in a grey suit by the main doors. He had a name badge that read MR TREETA – STORE MANAGER and he was fat in his middle, but not anywhere else, like he'd strapped on a fat-belt. He had grey hair streaked with black.

"Do you mind not mentioning this to my staff?" he

whispered to Donald's mum. "If they find out I've employed a ghost hunter they'll think I'm crazy."

"Fine, fine," Mum nodded, looking short-sightedly around her.

Donald tapped his foot in time to the lively music pouring out of the tannoy. It was very unlikely this place was haunted. This was a waste of time. But as he stepped further into the shop, his neck went all shivery and there was a heavy feeling in his head.

This was most definitely not a waste of time.

"Do you sense anything unusual yet?" asked the supermarket manager, anxiously.

"Erm." Mum scratched her head.

Mr Treeta stepped closer. "Things move at night," he breathed. "Bottles tip off shelves, pears roll over the floor, and –" he cleared his throat "– meat dances in the aisles."

Donald leaned against the potato shelf. He knew, without doubt, that the place was haunted, even though he hadn't seen a single ghost yet. (Apart from Jack, but he didn't count because he was outside.)

Mum rubbed her glasses on her sleeve.

"There's something disturbing here," she said, winking at Donald.

Mr Treeta took Mum's arm. "Let's talk in my office." Donald struggled to his feet.

"Stay here and have a look around," said Mum. "I won't be a minute."

As she walked away, strange blue and grey vapours ran along the ceiling above her. A mass of curling shadows trickled over Donald's feet and a sludge-brown shape seemed to melt into the tiled floor. Then a high-pitched whine filled his head.

Donald put his hands to his ears. This must be the most powerful, evil ghost he had ever not met.

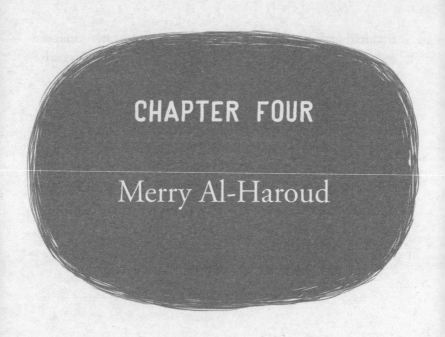

CHAPTER FOUR

Merry Al-Haroud

The whine upgraded to a howl, growing louder and louder until it seemed to fill every particle of the space. Donald spotted a fast-walking, sporty-looking woman in a black tracksuit trailing children of various sizes. It was Susie, Merry's mother. The smallest child, a boy, was dragging his feet, punching the shelves and howling like a crazy wolf.

And there, at the back, was Merry.

"Hey." Donald tapped her shoulder.

"Arrghhh," Merry yelled with such power that shoppers eyed them suspiciously. Merry's mother did not stop. With six children, her finely tuned ear meant she only intercepted when yelling was Serious.

"You're jumpy," said Donald.

"Don't creep up on people." Merry flicked his nose.

"Sorry. We're hunting ghosts."

"Really?"

"I can't see them properly, they've all lumped together. But I can FEEL them." Donald lowered his voice. "This place is at least a level nine."

"NO A WAY," said Merry, her eyes wide. (This was Merry's way of saying of GO AWAY mixed with NO WAY. She had stolen it from Donald, who'd got the sayings mixed up in the first place.)

"You said a level nine was so haunted we'd go mad with fear."

Donald nodded. "Yes, but now it's so busy the dead get scared off. This is a twenty-four hour supermarket. It must get properly spooky at night."

He paused to watch Merry's brother. The child was now lying on the floor, thrashing around like he was fighting invisible forces.

"He's possibly possessed," observed Donald calmly.

"Cut it out, Azeem," snapped Merry's mum.

Merry's parents had chosen popular names from different world regions to name their six children. They had:

Pedro (representing the Americas), age fifteen.

Carra (representing Australia and the Southern Hemisphere), age thirteen.

Merry (representing Antarctica, because no one knew any Antarctic names because who actually lives there besides penguins and scientists?), age eleven.
Oku (representing Africa), age seven.
Delphine (representing Europe), age five.
Azeem (representing Asia), age two.

Only the youngest four continents were in the supermarket that evening.

Just then, Mr Treeta and Mum came out of a side door.

"Why is she staring at everything?" asked Merry, watching April. "Are those ghost-hunting moves?"

"No, she's looking for me," said Donald. "She's as blind as a deep sea fish wearing very dark glasses."

"How can she have the second sight if she hasn't got eyesight?" asked Merry.

"You don't just see ghosts with your eyes," said Donald. "You feel them with your skin; you smell them, taste them, touch them."

"I only see them when I see them," said Merry. "But I'm not as talented as you," she added.

"Everything OK, Donald?" asked Mum, bouncing over.

"We've got company," he said.

"Level?" murmured Mum.

"Nine," said Donald.

Mum put her hand to her mouth.

Mr Treeta joined them and Mum smoothed her hair and put her palms together.

"Mr Treeta," she said, "your supermarket is extremely haunted."

"I knew that already," said the supermarket manager. "What are you going to do about it?"

At home, Mum got out her notepad.

"Any more thoughts about Bargainormous?"

The doorbell rang.

"Who could that be?" muttered Mum.

"Shouldn't you know already?" said Donald under his breath.

"Hell-looo? Memphis family? Are you back yet? I'm NEVER taking that child to the supermarket again."

It was Merry's mum, Susie. She placed a purple box on the table.

"I'm returning your crystal ball," she said. "I had a good look in it, but I didn't see anything except my nose. I definitely do not have The Gift. I'll have to do my job by the usual methods."

Susie had once been a historian. Now she made money by researching other people's family trees and ancestors.

Mum offered Susie a seat. "I need your historical knowledge. Do you know anything about the land where Bargainormous supermarket is built? Donald thinks we have a level nine."

Some people were sceptical about Mum's job. Susie and her husband, Ali, were not. Susie was particularly fascinated by the whole thing, especially when her work and Mum's collided, which it did often, as both of them were interested in dead people.

"Bargainormous was built on a plague pit," said Susie.

"A what?"

"This town was nearly wiped out by the plague of 1666. Lots of people died. It happened so fast no one had time to bury them in individual graves. They all got dumped in a pit, a mass grave."

"But why are the ghosts so cross now?" asked Donald. "They must have been down there for years, quite happy."

Mum squared her shoulders.

"There's only one way to find out," she said. "I'll go back at midnight."

Midnight, as you'll know, is a time when ghosts and spirits are at their most powerful. Donald always thought it was because ghosts like the void between today and tomorrow.

"You can't go back there at night," he protested. "It's a level nine, remember? You'll get possessed!"

"I'll be grand," said Mum stiffly. "You forget I've been doing this for years."

"But, Mum—"

"Relax," said Mum. "I'm a professional."

Later, Donald heard his mother on the telephone. She was speaking in a quiet voice.

"But, Estella, Donald says it's a level nine."

Estella Grey was also a medium. Mum had known her for years but they were not exactly friends. She was an expert on hauntings and an experienced ghost talker but Donald thought she was a bit of a know-it-all. She had a funny-shaped head that seemed to sit too far forward on her neck, like a snake. She was also head of The Believers, a group of professional ghost hunters. Mum used to be a member but now she said she preferred to work alone.

"I'm going back tonight, but I'm a teeny bit nervous. What do you think?"

Donald sat up. Mum rarely asked Estella for advice. The two of them had an uneasy rivalry.

"OK. I'm not going to stir up any trouble."

Mum always said that when she intended to do the opposite.

CHAPTER FiVE

The Plank and the Fire Escape

"I don't need a babysitter," growled Donald, scraping the last traces of strawberry yoghurt from the pot. "I'm eleven years old!"

"See you in the morning." Mum bent to kiss his cheek.

"Don't go," said Donald. "It's dangerous."

"Darling, thousands of people go to supermarkets at night." Mum tied her bootlaces. "It's not even midnight." She was wearing her black velvet cloak and black skirt sewn with hundreds of tiny mirrors. These were her medium clothes. She wore them to make her feel magical.

The ghost of Mr Thomas Jones appeared at the back door.

Yet again, this was an inconvenient time for him to arrive.

"Mothers know best, young man," he said. He was fond of Mum. He said she was like the daughter he never had. He adjusted his braces and stamped the mud from his boots.

I expect you'd like to know about him. OK, but I'm going to be brief because he's holding up the story. I promise you will hear more about him later.

Mr Thomas Jones was seventy-one years old (when he died), was Welsh, had long grey sideburns but no hair on his head, and loved to have long chats about vegetables.

"Now then, Mrs Memphis," he said. "Shall we have a look through the seed catalogues?"

Donald's mother smiled in a strained kind of way.

"Maybe later, Thomas, I must go to work."

"Mum! It will blow your circuits. Take me with you!"

"Shhh." Mum looked meaningfully through the kitchen door.

Cindy, the babysitter, was in the sitting room, watching telly. She thought Mum was going to tidy up her shop. Mum kept the ghost-hunting side of her business quiet. People could be funny about things like that.

"Be in bed by nine. It's a school night," ordered Mum.

"Mum."

"Goodnight, darling." Mum swept out of the kitchen, clutching her most powerful spectacles.

"Don't call me darling," growled Donald.

"I'd love someone to call me darling," mused Mr Jones.

"Hello, darling," said Donald impishly. He got fed up

with Mr Jones sometimes. It wasn't very relaxing having someone appear in your kitchen, though Mr Jones never came further than the doorway.

"Cheeky," warned Mr Jones, promptly vanishing.

Donald listened as his mother started up The Charmer (eighth attempt).

It was difficult being eleven. When he was sixteen, he would stride out of the house after his mother. He would go where he wanted. He wouldn't be stuck here, with *Cindy*.

The babysitter had a haircut like a Playmobil figure and a habit of crooking her head to one side when she spoke in her lispy voice. Right now she was wrapped in a pale blue blanket so only her moony face stuck out. She looked like a giant cocoon.

"I'm going to bed." Donald stuck his head round the door.

A news programme was talking about a museum in Dorset which had been burgled.

Donald thought if he was a burglar, he'd burgle banks and sweet shops. Not museums.

Cindy dragged her eyes away from the flickering screen. "You need anyfing?"

"Uh-uh." Donald backed away.

The first narrow flight of stairs led to a tiny landing. There were two doors. The first led to Mum's bedroom and the second to a small bathroom. Donald climbed up another tiny, steep staircase with bare creaking boards. The walls were painted white with cracks running through them, but Mum said the cracks were nothing to worry about, merely spirits trying to get in.

Donald ducked as the ghost of a large crow flew out of one wall and straight through the other. The house was built on a bird migration route. The alleyway had also originally been part of an old road, and cobbles could still be found in the garden. There was usually a trickle of ghosts passing through the ground floor. Every Saturday, on the old market days, Donald and Mum would get pedlars and farmers and the odd horse and cart coming through. These ghosts were so old they made little impression and were only often a silver shiver, rippling the air like a heat haze.

Donald's bedroom was in the attic. The roof sloped to the floor on both sides and he could only stand upright in the centre of the room. He had a narrow bed with three wooden boxes underneath for his clothes. He also had a tiny table for his TV and his Wii and allegedly for his homework.

The best thing about Donald's room was that the dormer window opened directly opposite Merry's window in the house next door. A plank rested on each of their windowsills, allowing them to travel from house to house. They couldn't fall because the walls of their houses met.

Merry's house used to be a vicarage and was four storeys high, with a thick oak front door and pointy windows. Fearsome stone gargoyles sneered from under the roof and spiked iron railings ran along the garden wall. The house was about five times the size of Donald's and it reminded him of a Christmas advent calendar with different things going on inside all the windows. There was always music or singing or shouting or laughing or cooking smells wafting out.

Merry shared her bedroom with her five-year-old sister, Delphine.

Donald crawled over the plank through the dark night and knocked softly on Merry's window. Nothing. He knocked again. The curtain had been drawn but chinks of light seeped out.

"Merry?"

The window pushed open and a small, cross face poked out.

"You broke my dream," it said.

"Hi, Delphine, sorry to wake you. Is Merry there?"

"I am now." A second head appeared. "Come in, it's freezing."

Donald crawled through the curtains into Merry and Delphine's bedroom.

Delphine, a tiny elf of a girl with long toes and dark eyes, was wearing turquoise pyjamas with a pink elephant on the front.

"Ghost Boy," she said. "Play fighting fairies with me?"

"Go to sleep, Delphine," said Merry, who was sitting on her bed, stroking her black-and-white cat, Sampson.

"I need your fire escape," said Donald. "Mum's off investigating the level nine on her own."

"She's insane," said Merry. "Can I come?"

"If you go with Ghost Boy I'm telling," said Delphine.

"Sneak," snarled Merry. "Snitches end up in ditches." She pointed to another window at the back of her room.

"All yours. It looks like I'm staying in."

Merry's house had long metal fire escape running from the attics, where Merry's brothers slept, down to the garden.

"Sorry about the ghost boy thing," said Merry, making a rude face at her little sister.

"It's all right," said Donald. "It's true." He paused. "As long as she doesn't think *I'm* a ghost."

He slid the catch and opened the window. The wind blew through his hair and made him shiver as he stepped back out into the darkness. All around the city, lights winked and blinked and the cold clouds raced overhead. Donald climbed down the metal staircase, finally arriving on the wet grass. He shunted over the fence into his own garden and wheeled his bike out of the shed.

He was free. Free as the wind scooting over the Arctic snowfields, free as the grass in the wild African plains. Free as the water in a remote Siberian river. Free! Free!

"Where are you sneaking off to, then, boy?"

He was not free.

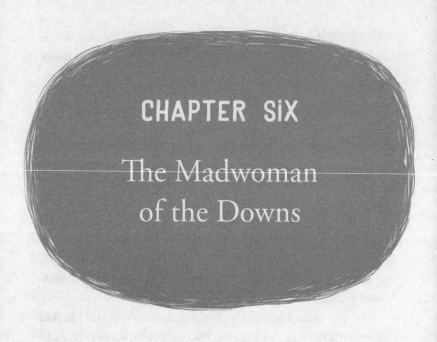

CHAPTER SIX

The Madwoman
of the Downs

Donald cursed as he smelled Thomas Jones's ghost breath.

"I'm off to football practice." Donald crossed his fingers behind his back. "If you play in the dark, you get better skills."

"Newfangled ways," said Thomas Jones. "Where's your footy boots?"

"My mate borrowed them," replied Donald, quick as a whip.

"Shorts?"

"Too cold."

"Half-time oranges?"

"Not in this century."

"You're never going to football," sneered Thomas. "What time is it? My watch has been broken for fifty years. It must be past your bedtime."

"Oh, get a life," said Donald quietly. Then he wished he hadn't. It wasn't fair, being cheeky to dead people. Weren't things bad enough for them?

"Don't tempt me," said Thomas.

Donald looked guiltily at his shoes. He wasn't usually rude to grown-ups. But there was something about Thomas Jones that brought the worst out of him. He tried to stop himself but Thomas Jones was annoying and Donald had fallen into bad habits.

"I feel sorry for your poor mother," said Thomas Jones. "You're always creeping off somewhere."

Thomas Jones mostly haunted the garden shed. He had been, in his day, a skilled gardener. Sometimes Donald would find a patch of disturbed earth that was either frisky badgers or Thomas Jones doing phantom gardening.

"When did you die?" asked Donald, trying to make up. Ghosts loved talking about their deaths (apart from his dad).

"Nineteen seventy-six," said Thomas. "Year of the drought. I was mulching the tomatoes when I dropped dead. Don't know why I've stuck around. The missus didn't. She died ten years before me; missed her like sunshine, I did. And as soon as I popped me clogs, I thought, Now then! She'll come visiting and wanting some beetroot. But not a sniff. I must have been a bad husband. But I would love to hear her sing again."

"Bye, Thomas," said Donald, pushing his bike through the grass.

"You still haven't said where you're going."

"That's because you'd tell Mum," said Donald.

"I love her like me own daughter," said Thomas. "I never had a daughter, nor a son. But if I had, I'd want her to be just like April. Interested in the past."

As Donald pedalled up the street, he waved at the little old ghost lady, standing, as ever, on the corner. A few minutes later he wondered again if something or someone was following, but whenever he looked round, there was just an empty road.

It was half past nine. All the houses had their curtains closed and the wind blew in his face. He sensed that Mum was in trouble already. He reached the supermarket car park in just under twenty minutes. He locked his bike to a row of trolleys and approached the brightly lit facade. He paused as the double doors swished open.

Leave, leave, leave, leave.

The chanting sounded in his ears and it felt much worse than earlier.

"For goodness' sake," said a voice in his ear. "Get the witch out of here."

It was Jack, the boy spirit from earlier.

"Do you mean my mum?" asked Donald, annoyed. "She's not a witch."

"She's channelling the ghosts," said the boy. "Make her stop before she gets possessed."

"I'll do what I can." Donald stepped over the threshold of the building, squinting in the lights.

The supermarket music was pumping from speakers in the ceiling. It was the sort of tune you forget instantly, the musical equivalent of air freshener, invasive and crude.

Mum wasn't in the fruit aisle, nor by the pet food, and Donald couldn't see her by the wine or the cheese counter either. But he felt compelled to stay away from the back of the shop. This meant he should go there. He followed the faint smell of fish. With every step it got more difficult to move, like he was walking into a warm blizzard.

PING! An overhead light blew, plunging his aisle into gloom. A young woman in black-and-pink stripy trousers dropped her basket and oranges rolled over the floor. Then one floated up to the ceiling.

"Gawd!" shrieked the woman. "Look at that!"

Then he saw a black puddle rippling and inching over the floor like a manta ray. It was Mum's velvet cloak. Donald trapped it with his foot and it curled up round his calves.

"I'M ONLY HAVING A CHAT," screamed a recognizable voice. "SPIRITS! DON'T FIGHT ME!"

Just ahead, Donald's mother flailed and swiped as she was pinioned to the glass fish counter by something invisible. Donald hid behind a mountain of cans. With great effort he drained his mind of thoughts.

Gradually, images began to appear.

There were hundreds of ghosts clustered round her. The swarming, clawing madness made him want to faint.

"Crikey."

The fish counter looked strong, but either the glass or his mother would break.

Behind him, Donald saw a mass of tins of chilli beans whirling round the air like a swarm of bees. Loo rolls were unravelling, bags of pasta were splitting and chocolate was melting on the shelves. A giant soup of food swirled around the aisles. Donald ducked to avoid a frozen plucked chicken which flew past on featherless wings.

The woman in stripy trousers gazed in astonishment as tins toppled, crisps exploded and packets of gravy rained through the air.

"This must be a dream," she muttered.

But most of the activity was taking place around Mum.

Donald couldn't go any closer or she'd see him and tell him off for sneaking out after dark. It's true! Mothers do not like to be disobeyed. Even when they are fighting off crazed ghosts.

Donald looked again and saw hundreds of the angry old spirits now whirling through the air. They wore rags and winding sheets and old-fashioned costumes. There were men, women and children and they were all very faint. In a few years, they might fade altogether. What made them powerful was the sheer mass of them.

"No dogs allowed," said a voice in his ear.

"I haven't got a dog," protested Donald. A huge security guard with hairy fingers was standing next to him.

"It's gone," said the security guard. "It was a big black thing." He looked at Donald. "What are you doing here on your own at night?"

"My mum's outside in the car; she can't come in. She's got a runny tummy," said Donald.

"Earrrhgg," said the guard. "The medicine aisle is over there." He didn't seem to notice the bag of frozen peas hovering over his head.

Then Donald had a brainwave and pointed to his mother.

"Have you seen the Madwoman of the Downs?"

They watched as Mum lifted off the floor.

"Put me down," she snapped.

"She's addicted to fish," said Donald. "You must escort her out. There's something about fish that drives her crazy."

"She sure is acting odd," said the guard, watching as Mum levitated up the glass and was placed on top of the counter. "How does she do that?"

"She's desperate to get at the fish," said Donald. "If you take her outside, she'll click back to herself."

"Oh, all right," said the guard. He squared his shoulders, put on a manly expression and shouldered towards Mum. Donald winced as his mother was dragged off the fish counter. He would not like to be caught between a sixteen-stone night security guard and the desperate anger of hundreds of tormented souls, but soon enough the guard had Mum marching down the aisle and out of the shop.

Donald breathed out. As soon as his mother had left the store, things seemed to calm down a little. The chicken flew back to its perch and no more cans exploded, but there was still a nasty feeling about the place.

"GET OUTTTTTT!" screamed a voice. "OUT! OUT! OUT!"

A gaunt spectre loomed over him, rags billowing from long yellowy arms. Eyes blazing with dead fury.

Donald held out his hand.

"What's bugging you guys?"

"I am the squire," howled the ghoul. "And you willll obey meeeeeeee."

Donald was not afraid of ghosts. After all, he spent nearly every Saturday afternoon listening to records with one. But this ancient spirit, with his mouldering face, his sunken eye sockets and his deep rage, was completely terrifying. He dangled closer and an icy chill wound around Donald's body.

"OUUUUT." The spirit's teeth fell out of his mouth and crumbled on the floor.

"I'll be off, then," said Donald, hurrying in the direction of the exit. Then more *things* were behind him, baying in outrage. Donald broke into a run, flying past an open-mouthed old woman, who obviously also had The Sight and was paralysed with fear. He flew past the tills and out into the car park.

"Told you it was spooky," said Jack the ghost, who was lurking by the cash machines.

Donald watched his mother climb shakily into The Charmer, start it up (third attempt) and drive away.

"What's the matter with the ghosts in there?" asked Donald, trying to calm himself.

"Dunno," said Jack. "They were pretty much completely faded, but then last summer, there was a buzzing in the topsoil and the lamps went all crazy and now the place is humming again."

"What changed?" asked Donald. Something Dad had

said was bugging him. But he couldn't remember what it was.

"They keep the place open at night now," said the boy ghost.

"I knew it!" said Donald. "The Nothings don't like it being open all the time."

"Nah," said Jack, scratching a poxy-looking spot on his neck. "It's quiet at night. Only a few people come. I don't see why that would annoy them."

"Do you know what's eating them?" asked Donald.

Jack looked uncomfortable. "You know, that phrase, *What's eating you*, it isn't a good thing to say to people whose bodies are underground."

"Sorry?"

"You know," said Jack, a tinge of pink in his grey cheeks. "Worms and things."

Donald slapped his forehead. "I'd better be *going off*."

"Please stop. It's not funny."

Donald backed away. "*Chill out.*"

"Still not good," said Jack. "We dead people are all pretty chilly."

"Got it!" Donald finally remembered what Dad had said. Drawing together all his courage, he ran full pelt through the entrance.

"Don't go back, they'll tear you apart!" cried Jack.

Donald hurried up to Mr Treeta's office, taking the stairs two at a time. He looked through the small square of glass to where the supermarket manager sat hunched over his desk.

"Who are you?" he said wearily as Donald went in. "Have you been shoplifting?"

"I was here earlier with my mum, the medium?"

"She made things worse," sighed Mr Treeta.

The squire materialized on the desk. He bared his brown teeth at Donald.

"LEAVE."

"Can you see that?" blurted out Mr Treeta, pointing at the spectre. "Nobody else can. They all think I'm mad."

"Course I can," said Donald. "It's the squire."

Mr Treeta raised his hands in despair. "I'm going to lose my job. My bosses cannot understand why all my customers are crazy and the food dances." He was a pitiful sight. With his desperate eyes, twisting mouth and droopy shoulders, he looked, Donald decided, definitely haunted.

"It's the music," said Donald. "It's driving them crazy. The ghosts have been acting up since you've been open twenty-four hours a day, right?"

Mr Treeta nodded. "I guess so. But I can't shut the store, can I?"

"They can't cope," said Donald.

There was a round grey speaker in the manager's room, blaring out the same tinny music that was playing downstairs.

"Where are the controls for the music?"

Mr Treeta pointed an unhappy finger at a small rectangular block of plastic sitting on a table.

Donald rushed over, avoiding the squire. He couldn't find the OFF switch.

"It's done over the internet," said the manager.

Donald pulled the wires out the back of the box and a silence fell over the whole place.

Then they heard a car starting up and the call of a night bird. Normal noises.

The great grey ghost turned to Donald and looked him in the eye. Donald felt a chill like an ocean wave pass through him. The ghost wrenched what remained of his face into something that might have been an ancient, plague-ridden smile.

"*Peace at last*," he said in a deep whisper. And vanished.

Donald felt instantly brighter. The horrible oppressive atmosphere had gone. Mr Treeta stood up, an air of energy about him.

"It's changed," he breathed.

"Let's check downstairs," said Donald.

Amongst the aisles, the remaining shoppers selected their goods. The fruit on the shelves gleamed; the meat in the fridges lay still.

"No more music," ordered Donald. "It was driving them barmy. How can they rest in peace if they're bombarded with dreadful music twenty-four hours a day?"

"I'll never switch it on again," said Mr Treeta. "I must pay you!"

"Send the cheque to my mother," said Donald. He put a finger to his nose. "But don't mention me."

"How did you know it was the music driving the ghosts mad?"

"It was something my dad said," replied Donald. "Music

is important to him because makes him feel less dead. He's very sensitive to it. So I thought really bad music played all day and all night would be like torture."

"Music makes your dad feel less dead? I don't understand."

"Don't worry about it," smiled Donald.

Mr Treeta shook Donald's hand vigorously. "Anytime you want a job, just come here."

"Wow, thanks!" said Donald, delighted. He looked at the clock on the wall. If he beetled off home now, he might just make it up the fire escape and into bed before Mum came to check on him.

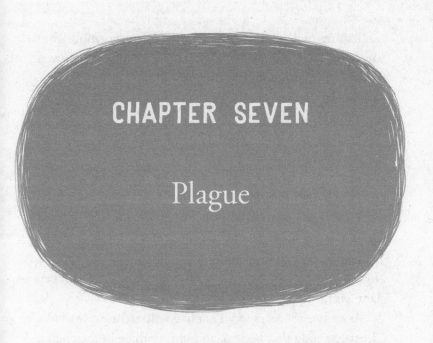

CHAPTER SEVEN

Plague

Donald's breakfast kept missing his mouth. The cornflakes fell off his spoon and made milky splashes on the table. Also his brain felt fuzzy.

"Mr Treeta sent me a bonus." Mum skipped into the room waving a cheque. It was over a week since Donald had sorted out the supermarket haunting. Mum was jittery because she was going to a Spirit Wisdom convention where she was doing a talk called "Negotiating with Wayward Spirits". Merry's mum was going up with her. Susie said she found lots of new business at these events. It seemed that people who were interested in spirits were usually interested in their family history.

"I thought I hadn't finished with Bargainormous, but Mr Treeta says the ghosts have settled." Mum scrutinized the amount written on the cheque. "Odd."

Donald decided to change the subject.

"Who else is going to the convention?"

"Everyone," Mum sighed. "Even Estella Grey, and I still haven't memorized my speech."

"Just read it from a card," advised Donald, who was now feeling seriously peculiar.

"How will anyone believe I'm a medium if I can't remember my own speech?"

"Mum, they'll love you," said Donald. "You talk to Nothings every day. Not many other mediums can say they claim child support from a ghost."

About twenty years ago, Dad had written one eighth of a Christmas song that had got to number three in the charts. It made so much money every Christmas that Dad had set up a bank account for Donald.

Donald stirred his cereal. He'd felt hot a minute ago, but now he was shivering.

"I won't be back until late. Go straight to Merry's after school and. . ." Mum's voice trailed off. "You're covered in spots!" She put her hand on Donald's forehead. "You're burning up!"

Donald felt his face.

"It can't be teenage spots; you're only eleven and not especially well developed. You can't be ill. What about the convention?"

Everything had been leading up to this day. Mum had a

new dress, new shoes and new tights. Last night she'd spent two hours locked in the bathroom with a spiritual barrier around her to keep out any ghostly intruders to practise her speech.

"Haven't you looked in the mirror today?"

Donald couldn't remember the last time he'd looked in a mirror. What was the point? He knew what he looked like. It wasn't like he got a new face every day. Besides, ghosts lurked in mirrors, and he saw enough of them as it was.

The doorbell pinged and Susie hurried in.

"Sorry I'm late, Merry's only gone and got chickenpox. . ." She caught sight of Donald. "Good grief, so have you!"

"Have I?" asked Donald.

"I'll cancel," said Mum, failing to disguise her disappointment.

"Why?" asked Susie. "Ali's at home looking after Merry. Donald can come over to us. Ali can look after them both."

Five minutes later Donald was bundled into his dressing gown and delivered to Merry's house.

Merry's face was dotted with tiny red spots and she scowled as Donald wobbled into her room.

"Why are you here?" she asked. "I want to be on my own."

"I don't want to be here either," said Donald. "You look terrible."

"Oh come on, you two," said Mum. "I thought you were supposed to be friends."

"I need peace and quiet, not friends," growled Merry.

She glared at Donald. "If you belch or fart in my room I will kill you."

"Death holds no fear for me," said Donald.

"Try and cheer each other up," said April hopefully.

There was a snort of laughter from the doorway.

"Don't worry, I'll stop them from killing each other."

Merry's dad, Ali, was forty-two years old. He had black hair and an on-off moustache. His family had moved to Bristol from the Middle East when he was two years old. He ran a taxi company and his fleet of taxis were all painted in special yellow luminous paint so they could be seen in the dark. Merry had begged him to choose a different colour, as the kids at school called the taxis "Dazzle Vans", which was embarrassing. But Merry's dad said the customers loved them.

"He'll give Delphine his germs," protested Merry. "Put him in Pedro's room."

"No a way." (Ali had caught the expression off Merry.) "It's like wild boar have been in there."

Donald, aching all over, got in Delphine's bed. It was pink and smelled of shampoo and farts.

Mum bent over him and kissed his spotty forehead. "Be good."

"Everything will be fine," Merry's dad reassured her. "Relax."

The door closed.

Donald knew he was never going to fall asleep in this pink stinky bed in a million billion years.

Donald opened his eyes. His sight was blurry as he read

Merry's radio alarm. Twelve oh three. He'd been asleep for three hours. He turned over and shot a cautious look in Merry's direction. She yawned.

"I was a little tired earlier on," she said in a sleepy voice.

"You had as much sympathy as a rabid rat." Donald pulled the duvet up round his shoulders. He was so cold he had the shivers.

"I'm boiling," said Merry, getting out of bed and padding over the floor in her red pyjamas. "Got to open the window."

"NOOO," said Donald. "I'll die of cold."

"I'll die of hot," snapped Merry.

"Lunch!" Merry's dad strode in with two bowls of soup. "You've both been asleep for ages. I've taken thirty-eight calls, played dragons with Azeem and put him to bed, and placated an old lady who was accidentally driven to Cornwall instead of the library." He looked delighted. "I should work from home more often."

Donald sat up. He had spots up his nose.

Spots on his bum.

Spots on the soles of his feet.

Spots under his fingernails.

Spots on his eyelids.

"Donald, I can't see any skin. You're one big spot," remarked Merry.

Donald muttered something very rude under his breath.

"No fighting," ordered Ali as he left the room.

Merry sat up in bed, slurping her soup. Donald tried not to listen to her swallowing.

Then it happened.

A huge ghost piled in through the wall and lifted Donald up by the scruff of his pyjamas. Donald struggled round, trying to see. The Nothing was dressed in a long brown leather coat and had a misshapen hat, with a long piece of leather that came down over his nose like a beak. He had rough black trousers and heavy boots. A smell of damp came off him like an unopened cellar.

He was definitely from the past.

"THOU HAST THE BLACK DEATH," he roared. "LEAVE THIS HOUSE."

"Oh, leave him alone," snapped Merry. "It's not that bad."

"You can see this Nothing?" Donald was impressed, despite everything.

"Definitely," said Merry. "He's the clearest ghost I've ever seen. I'm getting better at it. I think it's cos I hang out with you."

"THOU ART ALSO INFECTED, LITTLE GIRL," shouted the man. "LEAVE AND DO NOT RETURN."

He was a very strong Nothing. Donald slipped out of his pyjama top and fell back on the bed.

"Leave him alone, you bully." Merry's eyes were blazing.

Donald was impressed that she wasn't scared. Most people would be. Wouldn't you?

"And keep the noise down. My dad's downstairs trying to work."

"YOU ARE POXED," bellowed the man. "YOU MUST LEAVE THE CITY WALLS."

Donald rubbed his neck ruefully. "Who are you?"

"THE ENFORCER," replied the man.

"Go away," said Merry. "This is my house and you're dead. It is the twenty-first century and the plague has been eradicated."

"SILENCE, WENCH."

"It's chickenpox," Donald said weakly. "It's not that bad."

"I TAKE NO CHANCES. OUT, BOTH OF YOU." He went to grab Merry but she wriggled out of his grasp.

"What are we going to do?"

Donald was ruffled. "Dunno. Not many of them have the strength to lift people up." This was an unusual spirit. But then, most of them were unusual in some way or another, just like the living.

The ghost turned back to Donald, hauled him off the bed and marched him towards the door.

"How did you find us?"

The ghost paused. "The woman in purple, the witch, Goodwife Memphis, she came to the grave pits last week and spoke to us. She came again this morning and traded her coins for sweet flour patties. She spoke to her friend of your illness."

Donald groaned. His mother and Susie must have popped into the supermarket this morning for biscuits for the journey. This chap must haunt the place.

And now he was here.

"What's your name?" asked Merry.

"Henry," said Henry. "NOW COME."

The children were bundled out of the door and over the landing. Henry stopped at the stair gate. It was there to prevent Merry's youngest brother escaping downstairs in the evenings and raiding the fridge.

"Why is this fence here?" muttered Henry, fiddling with the catch.

"HENRY. YOU'RE DEAD," Merry shouted. "GO BACK INTO YOUR GRAVE AND LEAVE US ALONE."

"I KNOW I'M DEAD." He paused. "Do you think I'm stupid?"

"Then why are you bothering us?" gasped Donald. He really felt very ill indeed and did not wish to be dragged out into the cold.

"JUST DOING MY JOB." Henry cursed as the lever on the stair gate refused to open.

"You don't have to work when you're dead," said Donald. "That's the one good thing about it."

"DEATH IS NO BARRIER," said Henry. He cocked his head. "But this fence is."

At that moment, little Azeem, who had been enjoying his midday nap, waddled out of his room. With an expert flip, he had the gate open in two seconds flat.

"THAT IS A GIFTED INFANT," roared Henry. He grabbed Donald and Merry and continued to march them down the stairs.

"Look," said Merry. "Nobody invited you in. I want you to leave." She whispered to Donald, "Aren't ghosts supposed to leave if you command them?"

"There are no rules with ghosts," said Donald. "That's the only rule."

Merry's dad arrived at the bottom of the stairs. "You two look like death," he said, not spotting Henry. Ali never saw ghosts but he believed in them. Or at least, he said he did.

"THY OWN FATHER ADMITS IT," said Henry smugly.

"Dad, we're being haunted. . ." Merry could not continue. Henry had clamped a damp hand over her mouth.

"Bed," ordered Merry's dad.

Henry gazed at his rather elaborate dressing gown.

(Ali was making the most of working from home and hadn't yet got dressed.)

"Your father is a finely dressed man," he said, as Ali returned to the kitchen. "Is he a nobleman from distant lands?"

"No, he's a taxi operator from Bedminster," said Merry. "The dressing gown is from the M&S sale."

"You must not infect him," said Henry. "You are worthless children. But he has made it to manhood and must be preserved."

"Henry, look in the mirror," ordered Donald, for he'd noticed something.

"MIRRORS ARE FOR VAIN MAIDS," said Henry.

"Why did you die?" asked Donald.

Henry let go of them both. "HOW AM I SUPPOSED TO REMEMBER? IT WAS FIVE HUNDRED YEARS AGO."

"LOOK IN THE MIRROR," urged Donald.

Henry glanced in the mirror on the stairs. "Oh no." He put his hands to his face.

"Oh yes," said Donald, a little nastily. "Did you really think you managed to kick all those poor ill people around without catching the plague yourself?"

Henry's face and hands were covered in wicked-looking black spots.

"I MUST FLEE," he said. "I MUST NOT INFECT THE NOBLEMAN."

Merry and Donald winked at each other.

"And you must come with me," Henry added.

Merry and Donald stopped mid-wink.

"The nobleman would die of a broken heart," said Merry. "Besides, he has a special ointment to cure us."

"MAYBE HE COULD GIVE SOME TO ME?" said Henry hopefully.

"Sorry, Henry, there's no cure for being dead," said Donald gently.

"Henry, go," said Merry. "You're spreading the disease."

"I AM GONE," said Henry. He strode through the wall.

Safely back in bed, Donald lay back and folded his arms behind his head.

"We outfoxed that one!" He clicked his (spotty) tongue jubilantly. "What a thick ghost!"

"Are you sure he won't be back?" Merry examined each wall in turn.

"No a way," said Donald, plumping up his pillow. "He's history." He settled into bed, pulling the pink duvet over his chest.

Now for some well-deserved, deep, satisfying, uninterrupted, peaceful, refreshing, healing sleep.

Sleep.

Any minute.

Lovely.

"WHY ARE YOU NOT DEAD YET?"

"Hello, Henry," said Donald in dark tones. (The tones were Am and E, in case you want to run off and play them on your musical instrument.)

The spirit was standing at the foot of his bed. He had removed his nose cone and there was a determined look in his dead eyes.

"I HAVE RETURNED TO TAKE YOUR DISEASED CORPSES TO THE PITS."

"You've only been gone for two minutes," said Merry. "Give us a chance to die."

"Merry, let's show him the difference between the plague and chickenpox on the internet." Donald's head went all swimmy as Merry extracted her laptop from a pile of homework and powered it up.

"There is fire dancing in your box!" said Henry. "You are conjuring demons."

Merry did a quick internet search and found images relating to chickenpox.

"URGGHH," roared Henry, turning up at least five notches. "THOU HAST CONJURED THE POX!"

"Wait," said Merry, going to the NHS website. "Read this page." She was marvellously calm.

"I cannot read," said Henry. "Or write," he added bashfully.

"Didn't you go to school?" Donald felt a twang of fellow-feeling for Henry.

"Why would anyone go to school?" asked Henry. "It is for fops and the work-shy."

"I'll read it to you," said Merry, a little testy, for she was a great believer in the benefits of education. "Chickenpox usually clears up in a week to ten days. Do not go out until spots have scabbed over."

Henry looked worried. "Your box frightens me."

"It's called a computer," said Merry. "It frightens Gran too."

"We found this information using the internet," said Donald.

"A net to capture souls," breathed Henry. "I will leave you to die. I'm sorry I could not save your father."

He disappeared.

"Shame," said Donald, "I was beginning to like him."

"I wasn't," said Merry. "Now shut up and let me sleep."

"I just had a thought," said Donald. "I don't know if I should tell you or not."

"Out with it," said Merry, wearily.

"What if I caught the plague off the supermarket ghosts? What if Henry was right? What if this isn't chickenpox at all?"

"I'll kill you if you've given me the plague," snapped Merry. "But let's think logically. Can ghosts transmit diseases?"

"Not usually," said Donald. "But all ghosts are different. Some sing, some are silent. Some are nasty, some are lovely.

Some of them can throw you around, some of them can't come near you. There's no rules."

Merry pulled her duvet over her head. "Great," came her muffled voice.

"But I guess everyone who went to the supermarket would be at risk too," mused Donald.

"We'll find out soon enough," said Merry.

CHAPTER EIGHT

Bob Day

Donald lay in the bath, trying not to scratch his spots. For the first few days they'd hurt, then oozed icky stuff, and now were beginning to crust over. They itched like crazy, which was why Mum filled one of his socks with porridge oats, tied a knot and dropped it in his bath. It lay on the bottom like a rotting submarine, seeping out oaty slime. His spots no longer went:

ZING-ZING-SCRATCH ME-SCRATCH ME-ZING.

Instead they went:

ZANG THUD . . . ZANG THUD.

Which was an improvement.

It seemed that he and Merry had not caught the plague after all, though he had been worried for a day or so.

A flock of ghost pigeons passed through the shower curtain and flew over his head. There was a *splish* as one dropped a ghost poo in his bath, which fizzed in the porridgy water before it melted away.

Donald ran his tongue over the spotty roof of his mouth as a ghost mouse scurried on its tiny paws over the bath mat. Donald plucked his porridge sock from the oily water and threw it at the mouse. It squeaked in outrage. Not a ghost, then. Maybe now Mum would get a cat. Donald so wanted a cat. He wanted a cat almost as much as he wanted a dog. But he wanted a dog so badly he did not even want to think about it. He watched as the mouse scampered through the floor. So it WAS a ghost after all.

Donald could usually tell if someone was living or dead, but animals were harder. Especially insects. He checked out a spider, disappearing into a crack in the wall. Were those spindly legs real? Maybe spiders had died out years ago, and now all spiders were ghost spiders but nobody realized.

"Darling, are you OK?" Mum called through the door.

"Fine," said Donald. "And don't call me darling."

He heard Mum hovering, obviously wanting to chat. Her talk at the convention had apparently gone well.

"I forgot to tell you I saw Estella Grey." Mum spoke through a crack in the door. "She was in a very good mood because she'd just found a rare old spell book on the book stall. Anyway, she was SO interested to hear about your father. She thinks he's a new type of ghost. An SDH, or Super-Dense Haunting."

Donald scowled. Dad wouldn't like being discussed

by Mum's medium cronies. Especially Estella. He said he didn't get on with her when he was alive and now he was dead he didn't have to pretend to.

"She said it was extra-extraordinary to have a spirit that could hug you," Mum babbled.

Donald suddenly felt cold in his bath, but for all his supernatural powers he couldn't work out why.

"I always knew your father was dense," he heard Mum chuckling as she went into her bedroom.

Donald got out of the bath. His skin felt like it had been coated in butter. He felt deliciously itch-free, and when he dried himself, a couple of big scabs came off in the towel. It was all very satisfying. But most satisfying of all was when he picked a big bogey out of his nose and a crusty scab came out at the same time.

It was so good to be feeling a bit better.

It was so very very good to not be dead of the plague.

He thought guiltily of Dad. He hadn't seen him for a whole week. There was always the dread that one day, Dad wouldn't be waiting for him.

Once Donald was dressed, he felt hungry and ventured downstairs. He fancied a cheese sandwich, or maybe a glass of juice. Or perhaps there would be a pack of those mini apple pies in the cupboard.

Mum was waiting for him in the kitchen. She had undone her hair and it lay over her shoulders like a clean but mad hedge.

(I've never seen a dirty hedge either, but just imagine it, OK?)

"Do you want to go and see your dad?" she asked.

Donald halted. If he was the sort of boy given to saying rude words when surprised or otherwise provoked, he would have said them now.

"Holy farts!" he said. (It turned out he was that sort of boy.)

Had his mother ACTUALLY, REALLY, PROPERLY read his mind? Like a REAL, PROPER mind-reader? He believed that she was a little bit bad, actually completely awful, at the mind-reading side of her trade.

"I know what you are thinking," said Mum.

"Whoa," said Donald.

"You're thinking, how do I know what you're thinking?"

"Double whoa," said Donald, genuinely impressed.

"And now you're thinking, how do I know that you are thinking about how I know about what you are thinking?"

"Triple whoa," said Donald.

"I may be a bit rusty at my job sometimes," said Mum. "But I know you love seeing your dad."

"It's true," said Donald.

"There's a pack of apple pies in the cupboard," twinkled Mum. "Let's take them with us."

Donald stared at his mother. She'd done it again.

"What are you waiting for?" asked Mum.

The hug was a good one. Almost an alive kind of hug. Donald wondered yet again how was it that he could feel the prickly stubble on Dad's cheek and the soft frayed material of his old rugby shirt.

How could it be?

"Poor you," said Dad, releasing his son.

"I'm better," said Donald. "I've been worried about you."

Dad looked sad. "Don't ever worry about me. The worst has already happened."

Donald hesitated. Was this the right time to ask what had really happened to his dad?

But Dad was too quick. "Time to stop worrying and start listening to some tunes." He slipped an album from the shelf. "Today is Bob Day. First we will have some Bob Marley, a legendary Jamaican musician, followed by Bob Dylan, a legendary American musician."

"Dad," interrupted Donald, "why don't you ever play me new stuff? Not legends?"

Dad looked troubled. "This stuff is the foundation of your musical knowledge. You can't go through life without being able to sing along to 'No Woman No Cry,' or recognize a busker playing 'Blowing in the Wind'." He set the needle on the record. "We've got A LOT to get through. I can't pass over to eternal sleep until you've got all the classic folk, reggae, rock and roll, bluegrass, ska and punk lodged in your soul."

"But I don't want you to pass over into eternal sleep," said Donald. "Not ever. Not even if I knew all the legendary music there ever was."

Dad stroked his stubble.

"I'll have to go sometime," he said gently. "No ghost lasts for ever."

"Don't say that." Tears pricked Donald's eyes.

"But I don't plan to fade until you are very, very grown-up," said Dad, ruffling Donald's hair.

Donald swallowed. There was something else he wanted to say.

"Dad. There's some kind of spirit following me. It's been hounding me. It kind of slinks around on the edges of things."

Dad frowned. "Are you sure it's following you?"

"I think so," said Donald. "It's not always around, but it's dark, and fast."

This thing, whatever it was, had been following him for some time now. He'd first noticed it on the way home from school a few weeks ago – a shadow on the back of his eye – and he'd felt its presence waiting outside his house at night.

Dad took a quick look out of the window.

"Is it here now?"

"I don't think so. But it appears and vanishes without warning."

Dad took Donald's hands in his. "Does it make you scared?"

Donald shook his head. "No. It just makes me feel watched. It's like a psychic spy."

"Curious," Dad mused. "Let's monitor it."

"I mean, what's so interesting about me?" asked Donald.

Dad laughed. "Everything about you is interesting." He waved a record. "Now listen. This is Bob Marley and the Wailers. It's called 'Lively Up Yourself'." He set the needle on the vinyl disc and silently settled into his armchair. He shut his eyes and sang.

"Lively-up-yourself..."

Dad was the best dad in the world, even if he was dead.

On the way out, Donald saw the back of a tall woman, hurrying out of Dad's garden gate. He stopped and stared. Dad never got visitors; after all, he wasn't there. There was something familiar about her shoulders. Had he seen her somewhere before? The woman went off in the direction of the park. Donald wondered if he should mention her to Dad. Then he had a disturbing thought.

Can ghosts have girlfriends?

He jumped over the cracks in the pavement, singing mixed-up Bob songs.

"Hello!"

It was the old lady Nothing who waited on the corner. She had never spoken to him before.

"Er, hi."

The lady was wearing a pink blouse, a grey skirt and a flowery cardigan. On her feet were green old-lady shoes.

"Never heard you sing before," she said. She had a thick, lispy sort of voice.

"I've been ill," said Donald. "Now I feel better." It was funny how he never had any problem talking to ghosts. His words didn't get mixed up at all.

"I'm Ivy. I used to sing all the time. Then I lost my teeth and my husband told me I sounded like a singing lizard. So I stopped."

Donald noticed she had no teeth, just ghostly grey gums.

"He sounds like a mean husband."

"Oh, he was all right," said Ivy. "I'd go and see him if I

had my teeth. I'm too ashamed now; look at me. He's only down the road."

Donald thought for a few minutes. "Was your husband Welsh?"

"How did you know?" Ivy grasped his wrist. "We used to sing together. He had a lovely deep voice, a bass. He used to sing to his vegetables to make them ripen."

"Come with me," said Donald, and led her into his house.

Mum had a shoebox in the cupboard under the stairs, and in this shoebox were Things She Did Not Want But Could Not Throw Away. There were two wedding rings, a false eye, a lock of hair from Mum's great grandmother, a chipped china cup and a set of false teeth. Mum had found them under a rosebush many years ago. She kept them to remind herself not to eat too much chocolate.

Donald offered them to Ivy.

"Are these yours?"

Ivy shyly took the teeth.

"Oh my!" she said, and slipped them in her mouth. She gave a little jump.

"Thank you, little boy!" She sounded quite different now she had her teeth in. "You know, this used to be my house."

"I guessed that," said Donald.

"I'd best be going," she said.

They looked at the window. There was a faint tapping.

"*You always hurt the one you love. . .*"

"Tom?" Ivy's ghost clutched her hands.

"*The one you shouldn't hurt at all.*"

69

The ghost of Thomas Jones stood in the doorway, holding out a cabbage.

"*You always take the sweetest rose.*"

Ivy finished the verse.

"*And crush it till the petals fall.*"

Thomas Jones and Ivy fell into each other's arms and Donald looked away. He didn't like watching kissing, especially ghost kissing.

Thomas Jones looked up as Donald went upstairs.

"You're a kind boy. Thank you, Donald."

Donald flew up the stairs, happy that he had done another thing right.

Maybe he really wasn't so stupid after all.

CHAPTER NINE

Reintroducing the One and Only Danny Olini

"WAKE UP, DONNIE DAYDREAM!" Donald felt a jab in his ribs.

He was queuing for his school lunch and looking out of the window at some ghosts playing football on the school pitch. One of the ghosts, a long-ago headmaster wearing short trousers and a yellow waistcoat, had just committed a foul.

"Hey, Danny," said Donald, tearing his gaze from the pitch.

Danny Olini was built along the lines of a rectangle. His square shoulders and muscly arms looked like an adult's, even though he was only eleven. He wore fat white trainers, grey school trousers belted at mid-bum, and a chewed red school sweater. His heavy features and blood-filled earlobes wafted powerful waves of menace.

Danny turned his impressive head to look out of the window.

"Who are you spying on, Donnie boy?"

"Nothing," said Donald.

"One of your nothing nothings, I bet," said Danny. "One of your dead buddies?"

It was Danny's turn to be served by the school dinner lady, known by all the children as The Dread. She was a short, mean woman with no obvious chin and a deep hatred of children. She reminded Donald of a motorway lorry, mowing down everything in its path.

"I don't want any lunch," Danny said.

The Dread bared her teeth in a non-smile. She had dealt with Danny Olini many many times.

"Off you go, then."

Danny held out his plate.

"You said you didn't want any lunch," she said, eyeing him with distaste.

"I did," said Danny. "But my mother says I have to eat a school lunch. I'm letting you know I don't want it."

"Rude kid," said The Dread. She dolloped mash on his plate. She heaped up more and more, until it resembled a fallen cloud.

When it was Donald's turn, he said nothing. He was a great believer in not stirring up trouble. This was the opposite ideology of Danny Olini's.

"Why do you wind up The Dread?" asked Donald when they were safely sitting at their table.

"Because it is more interesting than not winding her up," said Danny.

"My mum says you are a bad influence on me," said Donald disloyally.

"I am," agreed Danny, chewing his mash with his powerful teeth.

(Note: most mash cannot be chewed – it is mash; it has been pulverized, flattened and pureed already – but this was School Mash, and therefore needed a good chew before swallowing.)

"But you wouldn't like me if I was A Good Influence." He spat out a globule of hard potato.

"What?" Donald was confused. Danny's mind seemed to work much faster than his.

"There are lots of Good Influences in our class, like Rory Yellam, and Addy Farmer. But you're not really friends with them," said Danny. "You're only friends with That Girl –" he shot a one-eyed look at Merry, who was finishing her lunch on the other side of the room "– and me. So you must be friends with me because I am Trouble, and therefore Interesting."

"I'm friends with you because you don't think I'm lying about ghosts," said Donald. "Everyone else does. Except Merry," he added.

"Ghosts don't exist." Danny licked his fork clean.

"So you think I'm lying too?" said Donald, disappointed.

"No." Danny belched loudly and winked at The Dread.

"You're a loony. You believe you can see ghosts. But that's OK, cos I like mad people."

Donald was lost. Did Danny like him or not? But before he could investigate, a dark shadow fell over him. His first reaction was that it was some dark spirit, or Mr Vellow, the head, come to complain about his table manners, but no.

"Out," ordered The Dread. "I don't want to look at your grimy faces a second longer."

"Shut your eyes, then," said Danny Olini, and raking up his belongings – his phone (forbidden), his wallet (empty) – he swaggered to the door.

Merry was leaving with her friends and Donald tried to hustle Danny out first.

But Danny Olini was not the sort of boy who could be hustled anywhere.

"Why, hell-loo, Merry Al-Haroud," said Danny, smiling as sweetly as he could manage.

"Hello, Danny Olini," said Merry reluctantly, for her friends were watching and sniggering.

"So, Merry. How is the family? Remind me of their names?"

"Mind your own business," said Merry, almost imperceptibly nodding at Donald.

Danny made his lips into a kind of beak between finger and thumb. "So where the heck does 'Merry' fit in?" he asked. "What continent do you belong to?"

"Oh, go and pester someone else," said Merry.

Donald frowned at her. This was Danny being friendly.

"You're not very merry, Merry," said Danny. "You should have been called Grumpy."

"If we're on to the seven dwarfs, I guess that makes you Dopey," said Merry sweetly. She made a *grrrr* face at him as she hurried off to catch up with her mates.

"She hasn't got a very good sense of humour," said Danny ruefully as he watched the girls leave the lunch hall.

"She does!" said Donald. "You weren't funny. You were teasing her."

"But I tease people I like."

"You also tease people you don't like. How's she supposed to tell the difference?" Donald felt like he was being wise. And one of the nice things about Danny Olini was that he didn't mind being told stuff like this.

"One day I'll win her round." Danny shot Donald a sly look. "You've managed it somehow."

"Aw, nuts," said Donald, feeling his cheeks grow hot.

On the way home, Merry caught up with him.

"Why do you hang around that hooligan?"

"I don't," protested Donald. "He hangs around ME."

"Danny Olini is the most annoying person I have ever known," said Merry. "I can't be in the same room as him in case I rebreathe air that has come from his foul mouth."

"Nobody's perfect," mused Donald.

"Why do you even speak to him? He freaks me out."

Donald smiled grimly. "It takes more than Danny Olini to freak me out."

He jumped as a shadow streaked across the road and darted behind a bin lorry.

"Did you see that?"

Merry shrugged. "You're freaked out now."

"It was some kind of animal." Donald peered up and down the road.

"Like Danny Olini," muttered Merry.

CHAPTER TEN

The Belle View Holiday Park

"I can't believe we're going on holiday." Donald did his run-to-the-kitchen-wall-and-jump-and-turn-round-in-the-air-before-he-smacked-into-the-other-wall thing.

"We need a spring break," said Mum, who was looking in the kitchen mirror and pulling out grey hairs. "I'm ageing too fast for my age and you still look peaky."

Everyone at school was catching colds and passing them round to everyone else, and then developing sick bugs, and giving them to everyone else too. Donald was good at avoiding illness (apart from chickenpox). Viruses looked a bit like see-through seaweed, though no one else could see them. He could tell if someone was going to vomit in the next twelve hours because the patches next to their nostrils turned silky and their third eyelid peeped through, like a sick cat's.

"But we never go on holiday," said Donald, suddenly suspicious. "We always go ghost hunting instead."

The only time they ever went anywhere interesting was if they were after a ghost. Mum always said that was enough fun for anyone and besides, they didn't have enough money to go swanning off to adventure parks and zoos. Also, she had the shop to look after. But last night, Mum had announced they were going to Dorset and were going to stay in a caravan by the sea. In February.

Mum, picking through her hair for a lost slide, looked shifty.

"Oh," said Donald, halting mid-bound. "We ARE going ghost hunting."

"Only a couple of little ones," said Mum. "Estella told me about a minor disturbance on the beach near the caravan park. She has requested my help, and what's more –" she shook her head in wonder "– the Believers' society are going to pay for our caravan."

Donald folded his arms. "Why do they want you so badly?"

Mum sniffed. "Maybe they think I'm good at my job?"

"Hmmm," hmmm'ed Donald.

"There's also a little churchyard ghost that needs settling. A private client. But the place we're staying has a swimming pool, a beach and an adventure playground."

"Shame Dad can't come too," ventured Donald.

"I couldn't survive a week with him in a caravan." Mum looked guilty. "Not that he isn't a very nice man."

Donald watched his mother as she spat on her finger and smoothed her eyebrows.

"Why did Dad die?"

A dense, deafening silence washed around the room. Donald could see it. This particular silence was like flour-water speckled with polystyrene pebbles, and it made three trips round the small kitchen before Mum cleared her throat.

"We were talking about our holiday!"

"I need to know," said Donald. "Was it very bad? Why won't you tell me?"

"Ask him." Mum couldn't meet his eye.

"You know he won't tell me."

"Not now."

Donald drifted upstairs, his good mood crumbling. Would he ever find out? Did something terrible finish off his father?

Once in his bedroom, he tipped into a headstand, his toes touching the sloping walls. He often had good ideas when he was upside down. But there were none now, just the sight of unwashed cereal bowls under his bed.

His darkest thought – one that he had never admitted to anyone, hardly even to himself – was ludicrous, but he wondered if Mum was somehow involved in Dad's death and that was why they never spoke about it. But it was so unlikely. Mum wasn't the sort to go round hurting people, even ex-husbands. All the same, he couldn't help wondering.

Something tapped at the window and Donald landed with a thud.

Merry pressed her face to the glass, squishing her nose and cheek, which made her look like a troll girl.

Donald released the catch on the window and watched her roll in and land on his bed.

"Hey," she said pleasantly. She was wearing a green tracksuit with a yellow flower pinned to her black hair. She made Donald think of daffodils.

"It's WAR over there." Merry settled herself on the carpet. "Pedro stole Delphine's gloves, so she tried to kill him, but kicked Mum by mistake, so Mum screamed at everyone and went to bed, leaving the dinner cooking. So Oku took over, but burned it, so Dad took over, but he burned it even worse, and then the smoke alarm went off and that woke up Azeem. So he started yelling too."

She let out a dramatic sigh. "How I long for peace."

Just then, Donald had a brainwave. (And he wasn't even standing on his head.)

"You should come on our caravan holiday to Dorset," he said. "There's three bedrooms so it wouldn't be icky. And there's a swimming pool."

"But you never go on holiday," said Merry. "There must be ghosts involved."

"Only a couple of small ones," admitted Donald. "Mum says there's a churchyard ghost and something about a beach."

"I'd miss Sampson, but I'd love to come," said Merry.

Sampson was Merry's cat. He was a violent thug and she adored him.

"Don't tell anyone at school or they'll think I fancy you. Which I don't," she added firmly.

"I know," said Donald. "I don't fancy you either." He smiled at her.

"Fantastic," said Merry, beaming. "How can we convince everyone?"

"Maybe they won't take much convincing," said Donald. "Mum says I'm less bother when you're around."

"My mum says I'm more bother when I AM around," said Merry. "I'm not really a bother. I'm just a child. Children are supposed to be noisy and break things."

"Like poltergeists," remarked Donald.

"Whatever," said Merry. "OK, when they all stop screaming at each other, I'll ask."

"I'll ask after she's eaten," said Donald. "Mum is always nicer after dinner."

Merry nodded. "All parents are like that. You just need to feed them to keep them happy."

The more Donald thought about the idea, the more he liked it. It would be great to have a friend to hang out with on holiday. And when he asked Mum, she was delighted.

"Brilliant plan, Donald. I don't know why I didn't think of it myself."

And after dinner, she emailed (even though Merry was only next door) to ask Ali and Susie and shortly after, a reply pinged back.

WHEN DO YOU WANT HER?

*

81

The February half-term finally came at the very moment Donald could not wait a millisecond longer. School had dragged on for twenty billion decades, with the teachers getting more and more grouchy and forgetting everyone's names, with their hair turning grey and their beards reaching their knees, and marking wrong things right and right things wrong, and even the chairs seemed to get more uncomfortable and prone to throwing children on the floor, and the school lunches had evolved into a tasteless grey-and-brown mush. (Until Danny Olini sneaked into the school office and ordered fifty pizzas on the headmaster's longstanding account. They arrived in cardboard boxes and the delivery driver refused to take them back, so Mr Vellow had no choice but to hand them round.)

But half-term did eventually turn up, just as the playing field popped with daffodils and the weather turned from very cold to just cold cold. The children ran screaming in relief from the school gates and the teachers sank into exhausted trances and had to be driven home by their husbands and wives and fed hot chocolate every hour.

And the very next day, Mum loaded The Charmer with luggage and food and extra duvets. It was raining so hard it sounded like hundreds of tiny samba players were having their first-ever rehearsal on the roof.

The Charmer did not start the first time.

She did not start the second time.

Nor the third.

Nor the tenth.

Nor the fifteenth.

"Van's not starting," said Donald pointlessly.

"Van's not starting," agreed Merry.

"Van will start," said Mum firmly. It didn't. It just made a sound like someone trying to laugh at a not-very-funny film and then giving up.

Ha ha ha.

Ha ha.

Ha.

"Van's not starting," Mum stated.

Donald wasn't worried. He'd dreamed about the caravan last night. Like most dreams, it was odd, and involved hurricanes and swimming pools, and Donald was certain they would get there somehow.

"Oh NO!" said Mum. "I KNEW I should have taken it to the garage last week. We're stuck!"

"Could Dad come and fix it?" suggested Donald gently, for his mother was sensitive about such things.

"Donald," said Mum, touchily. "Your father has hardly left his house for eight years. Also, he was USELESS at fixing cars when he was alive. Death doesn't turn men into mechanics."

"Oh," said Donald, disappointed. "I thought that was a dad sort of thing, fixing cars."

"Lots of mums fix cars too," said Mum testily. "Only I'm not one of them," she added.

"Got it!" Merry kicked the seat with glee. "We'll borrow one of Dad's Dazzle Vans."

"You think Ali would lend us one?" Mum asked hopefully.

"One of his drivers is off sick, so there's a spare," said Merry. "Let's go and ask."

Which was how, two hours later, Donald found himself bowling out of the city in a luminous yellow taxicab which smelled of peaches.

"Everyone is so friendly," exclaimed Mum. "They keep waving!"

"They're trying to get a lift," Merry told her. "Try turning the TAXI light off."

Donald watched as they flew past houses and flats and crowds of shoppers and workers. Soon they were leaving the city altogether and the rows of houses were replaced by hedgerows and gates and vast open fields.

"So healthy to get some good country air," trilled Mum, accelerating past an oil tanker farting out black smoke. She started singing a song about Mother Earth and Donald had to put his fingers in his ears so he didn't die of embarrassment. Mum had a singing voice like a fat old lady belting out carols at Christmas. Merry, sitting in the back seat, winked at him in the side mirror and plugged in her headphones.

The road they took, from Bristol to Dorset, was on a ley line, which, according to Mum, channelled the spirits. In the last half hour Donald had seen a road sweeper, a Victorian farmer, two horses, twenty-one badgers, and over a hundred hedgehogs. And all of them were dead. Donald was relieved his mother wasn't very good at detecting ghost animals, otherwise she'd be swerving all over the place. Just because something is dead doesn't mean you want to run it over.

"Nearly there," sang Mum.

"Really?" There was miles and miles of countryside as far as Donald could see, with low hills behind lower hills behind really low hills. Nothing indicated they were near the coast.

"There's a little church I need to look at on the way," said Mum. "A gentle sort of haunting, as hauntings go." Donald couldn't see the front of his mother's face, but her left-hand cheek and eyebrow looked guilty.

"It will be a nothing sort of Nothing," said Mum. "I'll sort it out in ten minutes."

CHAPTER ELEVEN

The Shadow

From inside the Dazzle Van, Donald watched his mother drift amongst the gravestones. She was holding out her arms and chanting, "Aaaahhhhhh". It was her classic ghost-hunting ritual and Donald didn't see the point of it. Ghosts either showed themselves or they didn't. All this stuff made her look silly. A couple of yellowy ghosts huddled under a gnarled old yew tree were following her progress with interest, pointing and sniggering. Donald put his hand over his eyes in despair when Mum tripped over a large vase of flowers.

Donald felt peculiar in graveyards because they reminded him that back in Bristol, in the churchyard a few streets away from his house, there was a grave belonging to his dad. To take his mind off this, Donald studied the church.

St Aubrey's had a square squat tower and an arched oak door. Mum said the new vicar, the Reverend Hattie Bisto, had experienced a series of incidents. First, her entire collection of vicar outfits had been hung high in the yew tree like giant black-and-white birds. The vicar had to get the Brownie pack to fetch them down. A few days later, Hattie's set of church keys had gone missing and turned up in the local policeman's underpants drawer. And when the vicar had found her white clerical collar cooked in a lamb casserole, she'd phoned Mum for help.

Now Mum wafted off round the corner of the church.

"What does the vicar think your mum can do?" asked Merry, who was playing Viper Attack! on her phone.

"Sometimes ghosts come back to earth for a reason." Donald opened the taxi door. "They either have a mission, their remains have been disturbed, or there's something wrong. Mum will try and find out what it is."

"So do all ghosts have problems?" asked Merry.

"No. Some of them just like hanging around for a laugh." Donald stepped out of the car.

Merry watched Donald read the gravestones. She knew she had only a teeny bit of the talent he had. Donald saw dead people everywhere, all the time. You'd be talking to him one minute, and the next, he would be gazing beyond you, watching Nothings or listening to some celestial conversation. And now, he had halted by a large square stone tomb, with a grouchy-looking angel on the top.

All of a sudden he was lying on the ground.

"Stop it," he shouted. "I'm not a thief."

"What are you doing?" Merry called, climbing out of the Dazzle Van.

"He says I'm here to steal candlesticks," gasped Donald, struggling to get up.

Merry tried to locate what Donald could see. Yes, above him, there was a change in the air, like salt dropping through water. With a thrill she saw an outline of a large oldish man. Gradually he became clear. He had a scrappy white beard and an unpleasant moustache. One boot was pressed into Donald's stomach. "GET OFF." Donald wasn't frightened, just cross. Merry ran to help but a strong wind whipped her face.

The Nothing glowered at her. To her surprise, she saw a glimpse of a vicar's white clerical collar and a long black coat.

"Another thief," snarled the vicar ghost through his beard. "Time for a lesson."

Merry was propelled along the path with Donald, her toes barely touching the ground. They were shoved round the back of the church, where old gravestones crawled with ivy and grave flowers rotted in heaps by the bank. A small door stood in the back wall of the church. The Nothing wrenched it open and thrust them inside.

"A night in the crypt will cure your thieving habits," he roared.

The door thudded shut and a key turned in a lock.

They were standing in a dark, low passage. The line

of light under the door showed bumpy stone walls and a sloping floor. Merry banged on the door and wrenched at the handle.

"Let us out!"

"Mum won't hear us, she's gone to the vicarage." Donald kicked the door in exasperation. "I can't see a thing."

Merry tried the door again. "This is the weirdest holiday ever," she said in a shaky voice. She was trying very hard not to be scared. But it is hard not to be something when you ARE something.

"Sorry," said Donald.

"I knew it would be odd. That's why I agreed to come," said Merry. "Let's go down here. There might be another way out." She started off along the dark passage. "Maybe this is the way to a crypt. They have crypts under churches."

Donald thought he heard a scratching noise behind him. Was something following him? He nervously palmed his way along the wall after Merry. "Aren't crypts where vampires hang out?"

Merry halted and Donald bumped into her.

"Vampires don't exist," said Merry firmly into the darkness.

"Ghosts aren't supposed to exist either," said Donald. "But they do."

The children shuffled on into the blackness, which, as they descended, grew more black. Blacker than the blackest black, like deep space without any stars.

"What about werewolves?" asked Merry casually.

"They aren't supposed to exist either," said Donald. "Like ghosts." All was quiet. Nothing was following him.

"What about demons and monsters and fairies?" asked Merry. "What about elves and sprites and poltergeists? And witches and wizards and warlocks and talking animals and. . ."

"I don't know," said Donald.

"But if something that doesn't exist does exist, that must mean that something else that doesn't exist could also exist," said Merry. "Like vampires, for example."

The passage widened as they met some broad stone steps, only discernible by a rogue slither of light.

Merry plunged down.

"Where are you going?" Donald tried to hide his alarm, but his worried voice echoed back at him.

. . .ing . . . ing. . .

"I'm finding a way out."

Again, Donald sensed some *thing* and looked behind him, but saw nothing but darkness.

On the other side of the wall, he heard a pair of ghosts arguing.

"*You let the pig out!*"

"*You told me to!*"

"*I never. Why would I tell you to let the pig out?*"

"*Why would I let the pig out unless you told me to?*"

They sounded like they might be husband and wife. As Donald climbed down the steps, the darkness seemed to creep into his skin.

The pig people went quiet.

There was definitely something following him.

It was close.

Donald's toes curled with fear. There was a taste of earth in his mouth and he had a vision of a shifting, bending shadow, chasing *his* shadow.

He knew it was The Thing. The Thing that had been tailing him these past few weeks. But how had it got here?

Donald drew himself together and went still. He could hear Merry talking quietly to herself, her voice getting further away. The thing behind him emitted an occasional deep breath.

The breath of something that didn't need to breathe.

Donald stood, wide-eyed, the muscles in his neck tensing. He thought of vampires.

Whatever this was, it was hunting him.

CHAPTER TWELVE

The Bear in the Crypt

"Merry," Donald called shakily. "Where are you?" He steadied himself against the cold walls as the darkness shifted around him.

No reply.

He tried to be brave. "I'm not afraid of you."

Which was a complete lie.

Sometimes he could sense what sort of Nothing was with him. Not this time. It was like trying to read a book with blank pages. Something shifted in the darkness beyond. A flash of yellow light. Small and oval-shaped.

Like the gleam of an eye.

It wasn't human.

Donald decided to move. Fast. He heard scrabbling on the floor behind him as he backed down the steps.

The fear *hurt*.

The yellow light flickered again.

He was trying hard not to panic but his legs felt weak and papery, as he reached the bottom and sensed he was in a wide, low chamber.

The thing was so close now, it was almost upon him.

There was no escape.

"Merry!" shrieked Donald.

"Oohhh!" she yelled back from across the room. What was wrong with her?

The thing touched his face and . . .

. . . licked him.

Donald blinked as the chamber was flooded with light. He was standing in a vaulted room with fat round pillars, and there, sitting at his feet and gazing at him adoringly, was . . . a huge black dog.

It was dead, of course. But that didn't stop its tail wagging madly when Donald looked in its yellow eyes. There was a smell of wet hair.

"It's you!" said Donald.

The dog sat and wagged; its tail thumped into the cold, dusty floor.

"You've shadowed me all the way from Bristol!"

The dog grinned, showing a row of wet teeth and shining black gums. He was so big, his head was level with Donald's chest.

"Why have you been following me?" asked Donald, and

the dog put his head down and looked up from under his considerable eyebrows.

Merry appeared by Donald's side. "I found the light switch," she said. "This is the crypt."

"Can't you see the dog?" asked Donald.

"What dog?" asked Merry.

"There is a large dog, like a giant Labrador crossed with a wolfhound, sitting at my feet," said Donald impatiently. "Try harder. I thought you were getting better at this."

Merry stared at the space. "Maybe I see something," she said. She wrinkled up her nose. "Have you farted?"

"That's the dog," said Donald. "He's been stalking me for weeks now. Only I didn't know what he was."

"Where is he? I don't want to trip over him."

"Here." Donald put out his hand and the dog levered himself up on his paws so his head was under Donald's palm. He felt rough, hairy and very doggish.

"Oh," said Merry. "Does he have yellow eyes?"

"Yes," said Donald.

"I think I caught a glimpse," said Merry.

Despite being imprisoned in a church vault, Donald felt tingles of happiness. He really loved how Merry saw Nothings too.

"Are you going to stick around?" The dog thumped the floor once more.

"I can see that," said Merry, pointing to the little flurries of dust coming up from the dog's tail.

Donald rubbed the dog's head. Mum had always said their house was too small for a dog, that they couldn't

94

afford to feed it and there was no time to take it for walks. But what about a ghost dog? It would require no food and clearly it wouldn't take up much space. It occurred to Donald his mother might not even see it at all, her skills of perception were so . . . unpredictable.

He could have a dog, and Mum might never know.

"I'm going to call you. . ." Donald gazed round the room, with its arched ceiling and stone floor. He studied a row of tombs in the corner and some plaques on the wall.

He would call the dog something important, something memorable. Something mighty.

"I name you Prince Shade."

The dog whined.

"You can't call him that, he'd get embarrassed," said Merry. "Call him a dog name, like Socks or Woofles."

"I can't call him Woofles," protested Donald. "That's a girl's sort of dog name."

"No it is not," said Merry, outraged. "I bet lots of boys have called their dogs Woofles."

"I bet they haven't."

"So you know every name every boy has ever called his dog, ever?" said Merry, squaring up.

"Maybe," lied Donald.

"Liar."

They fell silent.

"How about Mr Bristol," said Donald. "That's where I think he's from."

Merry shook her head. "You can't call him that. 'Bristols' is a rude word for ladies' chests."

"Really?" Donald was wide-eyed. "How do you know these things?"

The dog padded over to a tomb and sniffed. From the back, he could almost be a bear.

"Bear," said Donald softly, and the dog turned and looked at him.

"Bear," repeated Donald, and the dog gave a low woof and wagged his tail.

"Hey!" said Merry. "What was that? I heard something."

Donald grinned. "That was Bear."

The crypt was so cold, Donald could see his breath. Merry had wrapped her hair round her face to keep her nose warm. She also needed the loo.

"The only warm bit of me is inside my mouth," she complained. "It's all right for you, you're cuddling that dog."

"Ghost heat isn't hot," said Donald, tickling Bear's ears.

The crypt was lit by a single bulb. The room was full of dust and shadows and the air was still and stale. The children had been stuck inside for about an hour. They had spent half of that time banging on the outside door. Then they'd trailed back down to the crypt.

"I read about some people trapped in a cellar who got so thirsty, they licked the walls," said Merry, running her tongue over her lips.

"They would have been better off licking each other's tongues. At least there would be spit," observed Donald.

"GROSS," shrieked Merry. "I am NEVER talking to you EVER again."

"Or drinking each other's wee," suggested Donald, straight-faced.

"No way am I drinking your wee," said Merry.

"Then you'll have to drink Bear's wee," said Donald.

"Do ghosts wee?" asked Merry.

They watched as Bear started running along the walls, tail down and sniffing.

"Can't he just melt through the walls?" asked Merry. "What's the point of being a ghost dog if you can't melt through walls?"

"You read too many ghost stories," replied Donald. "Ghosts are all different. Some can do that kind of stuff, others can't." He thought of Dad. He hardly went anywhere.

"Bear followed you here from Bristol," pointed out Merry. "If he can do that, you would think he could do the melty wall thing too."

"Yes." Long ago, Donald had worked out the best way to keep on top of an argument with Merry was to agree with her. Merry liked arguing. She said it was because she had so much practice with her brothers and sisters.

Bear pawed at the foot of a stone plaque set into the wall. The inscription read:

REMEMBERING OUR STRONG VICAR
THE MOST REVEREND FRANK BIRD

Donald rested his palms on the plaque and pushed. Maybe Bear was trying to tell him something.

"Perhaps it will unlock a secret passage."

If this was a story, the stone would click and a trapdoor would open, and Bear would lead them out into the fresh churchyard air.

It did not.

"You've been reading too many rubbish books," said Merry. "No one finds secret passages in real life."

Donald thumped the stone in frustration and let out an unmanly squeal as something hairy and rat-shaped darted out of the wall and jet propelled over the floor. Issuing a series of frenzied yips, Bear set off in pursuit, chasing it round the walls and up the steps.

"Was that a ghost rat or a real rat?" breathed Merry.

"Real," said Donald, watching as Bear vanished up the passageway.

"Better a live rat than a dead vampire," said Merry, glancing again at the tombs.

Donald was fed up now. How long before the stupid Nothing let them out? His throat was dry. How long before they'd have to start licking the walls for moisture?

"I dare you to lie on the tomb," said Merry.

"Why would you make me do that?" asked Donald. "Aren't things bad enough?"

"I'm bored," replied Merry. "It would be entertainment."

"I'd wake up the vampires," said Donald.

But because he had nothing else to do, and maybe because he wanted to impress Merry, he approached the tombs. There were three of them ranged against the back wall, each one a large stone box. The first tomb was bigger than the others, with ornate carvings of leaves and flowers and odd-looking animals.

Donald put his hand on the stone lid. He sensed no Nothings.

Or did he? A cool draught ran up his sleeve and over his arm. Goosebumps prickled his skin. There was a long triangular gap between the lid and the top of the coffin, like it had been opened and not shut properly.

There are no such things as vampires, Donald told himself. Really. No. Such. Thing.

Donald could smell newly mown grass, and it was coming from the open seam in the coffin.

He knocked on the lid.

"Stop," hissed Merry. "Are you insane? I was only joking."

The fresh, grass-smelling air must be coming from outside. Donald tested the lid and it moved a fraction.

"Vampires," said Merry warily. "Vampires, vampires, vampires." She edged to the steps.

Donald thumped the lid with his fist. "THERE ARE NO SUCH THINGS AS VAMPIRES."

But as he spoke, he heard a dull thudding coming from inside the tomb.

He stepped back.

"What was that?" demanded Merry. "Come on, Mr Supernatural. WHAT WAS THAT?"

Bear bounded up to the tomb, sniffing as enthusiastically as if there were a whole family of rodents in there.

A ghost? A trapped spirit? But Donald hadn't got The Feeling.

This was something different.

"I'm properly scared," admitted Merry.

"Me too," said Donald, remembering he was supposed to be not scared of ghosts.

A blast of fresh air hit his face. From inside the tomb there came another thump and a muffled yelp.

Bear scrabbled at the base of the tomb and Donald and Merry watched with frozen horror as the lid began to move.

"Oh no," said Merry. "Donald. Move."

But Donald couldn't. Images of vampires were flashing through his mind. Pale-faced men in cloaks with bloody mouths. Sleek women in black dresses with pointy fangs.

The lid shuddered and juddered and there was a grunt.

"Quick, sit on the lid so it can't get out." Merry raced over and they began heaving against the lid. But as they pushed, a pale hand came thrusting out of the gap.

"Eek," screamed Merry, pushing harder.

"OUCH," shouted the thing in the tomb.

"Arrgghh," Merry gave it an almighty shove.

The hand was pale and soft-looking, with silver rings dotted up the fingers. One of them had a star design.

Donald's jaw fell open. "STOP." He dragged Merry back. "You're hurting her."

"Yes you are!" came a voice from inside the tomb.

"I don't care. It's undead. It wants to suck our blood,"

shrieked Merry.

The stone lid slid open and a dusty-haired figure rose out of the darkness within.

"It's not the undead, it's my mum," said Donald.*

---

* **WARNING**. Do **NOT** repeat this sentence when you see your mother first thing in the morning.

CHAPTER THIRTEEN

The Dead Rev

"Here you are," said Mum, a cobweb hanging from her ear. She sucked her fingers where they'd got pinched in the tomb. She clambered out, one leg at a time. "I've been looking for you for ages. That dratted man wouldn't tell me where he'd put you."

"You saw the ghost vicar?" asked Donald.

Mum flicked a spider from her velvet coat. "His name is the Reverend Frank Bird. He can't stand the new vicar. He says her sermons make him turn in his grave, so he's making her life a misery. Then I got worried about you two but he just vanished. An old lady ghost in the graveyard told me the Dead Rev always shut naughty children in the crypt, and she showed me this secret tunnel."

"You saw her too?" Donald was impressed. Maybe his mum really was good at this after all.

"Sorry, Mrs Memphis," said Merry, hopping from leg to leg. "But we've been in here for ages. You said this was a rescue?"

"Sorry, Merry," said Mum. "Follow me." She put one leg back in the tomb. "This is playing havoc with my tights."

"We go through the tomb?" asked Merry.

"Uh-huh," said Mum.

Merry screwed her mouth into a knot. "What about the dead bodies?" she said.

"There aren't any," said Mum.

Bear leapt into the tomb beside Mum with a dusty billow of air.

"What was that?" she asked. "I sensed something."

"Can't you two go out first, and then let me out through the door?" pleaded Merry.

Mum shook her head. "I'm not leaving you on your own. If the vicar comes back, he might be a tiny bit alarming."

Merry sniffed a particular sniff. "I see."

Donald looked up. Merry only ever sniffed that particular sniff on very rare occasions. It was the sniff she sniffed if she was trying not to cry.

"Merry doesn't like small spaces," explained Donald.

"Nor do I," said Mum. "But sometimes you have to be brave and get out of your comfort zone."

Merry bristled.

"She is brave," said Donald quickly. "And being stuck in a haunted cold dirty crypt for over an hour is out of everyone's comfort zone."

"Come along, we'll be out in a jiffy." Mum held out her hand.

"I Am Not Going In There," said Merry, and sniffed again.

Donald knew how hard Merry was finding this. She was a Good Girl and the sort of person who usually did as she was asked.

Unless it was crawling into a tomb.

"Got it," said Donald. "I'll go through the tomb, find the Dead Rev, get the key and unlock the door."

"What door?" asked Mum.

"The door into the crypt," said Donald.

"I don't want to let you out of my sight," said Mum.

"I'll be fine," said Donald, climbing into the tomb.

"Don't be long," ordered Merry.

There was a large hole in the bottom of the tomb. Donald climbed down narrow steps which took him into a low round tunnel. Soon he could see nothing at all and could only fumble along the walls. He didn't like to think of the weight of the church above him. And despite his bravado, he had no idea how he was going to find the ghost of the mad vicar and get the keys off him. But before he could worry too much, he saw a greyish light up ahead.

Thirty seconds later, under the watchful eye of a marble cherub, Donald was climbing out of a tomb, breathing fresh, damp air and screwing up his eyes against the light.

"Child! Descend! Cease your infantile entertainments."

A round-eyed woman in a black dress came haring over the grass.

"An inexpedient activity," she said. "These are the precious vestibules of the remains of the adored deceased." She had black curly hair cut in a bob and wore pink lipstick. She looked about thirty or sixty. Ancient, anyway. "These constructions present a hazard to your earthly body." She wagged her finger at him. "In addition, your action is disrespectful and hooligan."

Was she telling him off? Donald wasn't sure. Either way, people on rescue missions should not get told off. He noticed the woman was wearing a white collar that went round the front of her neck. This must be the real living vicar of St Aubrey's. The one who was having all the trouble. He felt his old trouble, the fear of talking to grown-ups, start to creep up his throat and paralyse his tongue.

Donald held out a grubby hand and wiggled his tongue in his mouth. "I'm Donald Memphis, April the medium's son. The ghost of the Reverend Frank Bird has locked my buddy in the crypt. She's too chicken to come through the tomb. Mum's down there too. Do you have a key?"

There! Beautifully done. No stammering or waffle. He was a master of speech.

The vicar came very close to him and bent low, so she was looking directly in his eyes.

"I am the Reverend Hattie Bisto. Donald Memphis, the supernatural phenomena to which you refer does not exist."

Bear chased a bit of grass over the path in front of her.

Sometimes you just had to be a bit pushy with grown-ups.

"Where's the key? April Memphis and Merry are shut in the crypt." After that rather good sentence, he needed to stick his tongue out to give it some air.

The vicar raised her arms.

"Such trickery and rudeness from one so recently sprung from the womb!"

"Eughhhh." Donald took a step back. He gave the vicar a searching look. "You, you, I – I invited my m-m-mum here, yeah?"

RATS. He was losing it.

The vicar looked shamefaced. "Stronger souls would have consulted the bishop, it was a foolish whim and. . ."

Donald waved his hand. "Please," he blurted out. "Can't you just come and look?"

"Of course."

As they walked among the graves, Donald had to listen as the vicar droned on and on about the impossibility of ghosts and how he shouldn't be thinking about them but instead should be climbing trees and building dams. At least, he thought that was what she was saying. The words fell out of her like heavy rain.

His words were more like ketchup. They wouldn't come for ages and then they'd come in a massive dollop and make a mess.

"Your mother is having a subterranean exploration that went amiss?" She spoke like a head teacher at an assembly of head teachers about using long words.

"My friend needs the loo," said Donald. But the vicar seemed to be more interested in him.

"You believe in the non-existent phenomena known popularly as 'ghosts'?"

"Uhmm, sort of," said Donald, because it felt safer than to give a yes/no answer at this stage. He wondered why the vicar had invited Mum here if she didn't believe in Nothings. They walked through the empty church. It smelled of polish and flowers and dust.

"But your ghost has lost the plot," he ventured.

Again the vicar hesitated. "What criteria prompted that unacademic sentence?"

"I saw Frank Bird. He looked well mean. He threw us in the crypt. Pretty savage timeout if you ask me. It's creepy down there."

The Reverend Hattie Bisto swung round. "I am on the margins of distress," she said, her round eyes becoming even rounder.

Donald was itching to go and rescue the others but the vicar was in no hurry. She led him down the aisle to the back of the church, taking every opportunity to explain at length the history of the paintings, and the stories behind the carved wooden thingummies in the roof.

"This area is known as the nave," she smiled. "See how smooth the floor has become? Worn by countless faithful feet."

Donald had an image of Mum and Merry trapped and huddled together in the dark under his feet.

"Merry REALLY needs the loo," he said in desperation.

Ignoring him, the vicar opened a door in a wood-panelled wall.

"This is where we house the vestments," she smiled. "And is therefore known as the vestry."

The room had an arched ceiling, a pretty stained glass window and wood-panelled walls. Racks of black gowns and choir surplices hung along one wall. Bisto went to a cupboard and drew out a large black book. As she flicked through the pages, he couldn't help noticing another book, a fat, dusty green tome entitled:

EXORCISM

Despite everything, Donald shivered. Exorcism was something which was done to get rid of ghosts for ever. Something he knew vicars did from time to time.

"Is this the spirit you encountered?" Hattie showed him a black-and-white photograph of a smiling priest. He had round cheeks and no hair.

"No," said Donald. He took the book and flicked through old photographs of choirs and weddings and vicars and stopped when he reached an old creased photo of a thin, ferocious-looking vicar standing next to some tall candlesticks. He wore a long black coat with silver buttons.

"That's him," he said, passing back the book.

Bisto gave him a very strange look.

"The old Australopithecine," she sighed. "I knew it was Bird."

"Wow," said Donald.

Bisto put her hand on his shoulder. "For what reason did you make that exclamation?"

Donald thought. It was a hard thing, telling grown-ups the truth. If you weren't careful, you could end up sounding rude.

"You didn't use long words, apart from that Australia thing."

"Aus-tra-lo-pith-i-cine. An early species of hominid," said Hattie. "Somewhat at odds with creationism, but hey ho."

At once a whispering sound filled the room and the gurning ghost of Frank Bird materialized before them. He was wearing the same coat as in the photograph, only the moths had got at it and it was a bit holey around the armpits.

"'Tis TRUE," he roared, the bristles of his beard sticking out like twigs. "She speaks like a druid! None of the flock can understand her words. She twists and wrings them like sodden laundry!"

"Chill," said Donald, holding up his hand. "I'm on it."

"Stay away from my candlesticks. . ." Frank Bird melted away as fast as he had arrived.

Hattie Bisto hadn't noticed a thing, though Bear had backed into the corner with his tail between his legs.

"Long words?" She was watching Donald expectantly. "The English language is a vehicle for truth, light and beauty."

"But that's no g-g-good if no one can understand you," said Donald, going pink. This felt like being rude. And even worse, rude to a vicar. No one was rude to vicars, not even Danny Olini. Probably.

"I credit my flock's cognitive powers!" said Hattie in a less friendly voice.

Donald felt very awkward. "You make words go round in circles instead of straight lines. I do it myself. Only not on purpose."

Hattie took a sharp breath. "Humility, Hattie," she muttered. "From the mouths of babes."

"Can we rescue my mum now?" Donald reminded her.

The vicar smoothed out her cassock. "I will humour your childish whim."

"Ace." Donald put his thumbs up. Now for the glorious rescue. The women in the cellar would be overflowing with thanks. Merry would smile at him and Mum would promise him sweets.

"I'm back!" Keys held aloft like an emblem of freedom, Donald presented himself, a shining liberator in the gloom of the melancholic sepulchre.

Whoops, I mean he arrived in the crypt, jangling the keys. Hattie's way of talking is catching. Why don't you try it out?

"About blimmin' time!" said Merry. "I was going to have to wee behind the tomb. Let's get out of here."

"Well done," said Mum as they made their way up the steps. "Did you get the keys off the mad vicar?"

"Which one?" asked Donald, grinning.

Hattie arrived at the top of the steps.

"Sorry about this, Vicar," trilled Mum. "We got a little waylaid. Your Frank Bird is quite a problem."

"Frank Bird," whispered Hattie. She shook herself. "Come. The discussion of unearthly beings should take place above ground." She looked meaningfully at Donald. "And out of the earshot of tender babes."

"It's OK," said Donald. "I'm not scared of ghosts. I see them everywhere."

"Really?" The Rev Hattie Bisto looked like she was about to launch into a speech, but a growl from Merry made her walk on. Back outside, Merry handed Donald her phone as she scooted off to find a tree.

"And now," said Hattie. "About our supernatural guest. . ."

And all at once the Rev Frank Bird was there again, swirling in the doorway to the crypt. His old eyes were so pale Donald could see right through them. The ghost glared down at Donald, and Bear stood reassuringly close.

"You," he roared.

"Me?" said Donald, looking wildly round for his mother. He needed adult backup. Yes, Mum could see the Dead Rev too! She was coming over.

"You must tell that female to speak plain in my church, or else my congregation will go elsewhere. Already I see them on holy days playing with the pigs' bladders." His worm-like lips contracted in anger.

"Football," said Donald. "Lots of people play footie on a Sunday."

"And visiting barns to purchase furnishings for their

111

hovels." A tuft of his beard seemed to float towards Donald.

"That will be Ikea," said Donald, batting the beard away.

"And worst of all –" the old ghost visibly shuddered and a bit of his robe fell off "– they flock in droves to the big mirror and watch unholy visions."

"The cinema," said Donald.

"They SHOULD BE IN CHURCH," roared the Rev Frank Bird. "But the she-vicar drives them away."

"I don't think you can blame her," said Donald reasonably.

"I CAN," roared the ghost. "Tell her to speak plain or I will continue to plague her."

Mum stood next to Donald, her cheeks glowing with excitement. "I think he likes you."

Hattie Bisto was watching Donald, wide-eyed.

"Is he possessed?" she asked Mum. "Should I enact an exorcism?"

"No and no," said Donald crossly. "I'm talking to your ghost. Frank Bird. The one you don't believe in."

"Oh, him," said Hattie. She did her shifty look again. "He distrusts me. I fear it is due to my gender."

"What?"

"Because I am a female vicar," explained Hattie.

"It's not that," said Donald, feeling awkward. Was he going to have to go over it all again? Then he noticed the writing on Merry's mobile phone.

Connecting People.

112

Bear, sitting quietly in the doorway of the church, gave him a reassuring wag.

"It's about how you connect with people," said Donald.

A dreadful smile cracked the face of the Rev Frank Bird. "GO ON, BOY!"

Hattie loosened her collar. "You mean the jumble sale committee?"

Donald wondered for the billionth time how grown-ups could be so thick.

"Frank Bird says you've got to talk more simply- er," he said.

Hattie squared her shoulders. "I tell you, I tell YOU, FRANK BIRD, if you are present –" she turned in the opposite direction to the old ghost and shouted at a surprised-looking robin "– I will not talk down to my flock."

"WHAT FLOCK?" screeched back old Frank, waving his bony arms in rage.

"Don't talk down to them, talk TO them," said Donald. "Not to yourself," he added quietly.

Hattie swallowed. "I feel disturbed," she said. "I wonder if I am, in a small way, guilty of needlessly enriching my vocabulary with glib notes." She rubbed her chin.

Donald now felt very bad indeed. How could he tell someone how to speak when he could barely string a sentence together?

"Well done, boy. But stay away from my candlesticks."

The ghost of the Reverend Frank Bird shuddered, and his beard became the dead grass growing out the side of the wall and his fingers became the grouting between the stones.

"Look." Donald pointed as a pile of leaves were swept up and whirled in the air. The leaves flew up the walls of the church and poured over the clock tower. The bell sounded a deep mournful clang and the leaves blasted out over the sky and scattered, falling like tree rain.

"A sign?" whispered Hattie, picking a leaf from her curls.

"No, a ghost," said Mum, firmly taking charge. "And that was a Dramatic Exit."

Dramatic Exits, Donald knew, were something ghosts did when they finally decided to quit hanging around – or in other words, when they gave up the ghost.

Mum took Hattie's hand. "I think your ghost is settled. I'll put your bill in the post. Just call me if there's any more trouble."

"I will enact some changes," Hattie replied.

"Thanks for the tour of the church," said Donald, and gave her a half wave.

Hattie gave him a penetrating look.

"You are special," she said. "You see much more than most. I wondered if it was true."

Donald swapped glances with Mum.

Hattie took his wrist. "I'm glad to have met you, Donald Memphis. Your mother informs me you are beach-ward bound on a major investigation."

"She did?"

"Remember, if there is ever an hour when you need assistance, I'm here." There was a look of deadly seriousness in her eyes that Donald hadn't seen before.

"Er, thanks," said Donald. He couldn't imagine ever

needing to ask Hattie Bisto for help. She couldn't even see the Nothings.

Then, checking that Mum wasn't listening, Hattie drew him aside. "There is something very disturbing by the coast. Something that you might see, but other people can't. None of us understand it. But we might be able to help you."

"Sure," said Donald. What was the woman on about?

"Remember," said Hattie. "Stay in touch."

Merry reappeared. "Can we go now? I'm ready for the normal-holiday bit now."

CHAPTER FOURTEEN

The Belle View Holiday Park (it really is this time)

Sorry, sorry we're finally here. Journeys are always delayed for some reason and the Dead Rev held everything up. Blame the Nothings, not me.

Mum drove the luminous yellow taxi up a smooth driveway, flanked with perfectly pruned bushes and sweetie-coloured flowers. They passed under the holiday camp arches.

Belle View Holidays

The air above the car park was a mass of birds, alive and dead, all fighting and bickering and searching for chips.

Mum went off to collect the key and Donald surveyed their surroundings as Merry dozed in the back of the taxi.

Dirty-white caravans with orange stripes were arranged in tight rows. They were about twelve metres long and covered the whole park apart from the vast octoid* "Fun Centre". Donald wondered which caravan would be theirs and hoped it wouldn't be the shabby one with a dent in the side, backing on to the car park.

A loud rumbling filled the air, making the gulls shriek. It was like thunder, but not quite. More like thunder's mysterious cousin. A second rumble was so loud it made the biscuits buzz on the dashboard.

Bear whined.

"What was that?" asked Merry without opening her eyes.

Donald supposed it was some far-off explosion. The noise grumbled on.

"This isn't what I had in mind when I thought of going on holiday," said Merry sleepily. "I thought we'd be running around in the sunshine, eating ice cream and laughing insanely at each other's jokes."

But then Mum came racing back.

"That's ours!" she shrieked, pointing at the shabby caravan with the dent. "This is SO exciting! And the thunder just adds to the adventure."

She unlocked the door and flung it open.

---

* Note: "Octoid", as a word, does not exist. Donald made it up to describe a circular building with eight offshoots. It is a good job I am here to interpret. That's OK. Don't mention it.

117

"Go explore."

Eleven seconds later they had seen every inch of the caravan. There were:

Three tiny bedrooms.

A sitting room and kitchen rolled into one (or a sitchen, as Donald would say).

Two loos (tight fit).

One shower.

Approximately thirty-five ants (not the biting sort).

No ghosts.

"So much space!" Flinging out her arms in joy, Mum knocked a cup off the shelf.

The rumbling had stopped and Donald went to unpack. He heard Merry humming in her room a couple of centimetres to the left. He stowed his bag of clothes in the cupboard and put his gorilla, Sir Isaac Newton, on the bed. He looked at the orangey walls, the scuffed carpet and his teeny tiny bed with the brown duvet.

It made him think of a giant cough lozenge and there was a taste of cloves in his mouth.

Something (probably living) landed on the roof and started scratching. Donald opened the window to investigate and was met by two things.

The first was an unexpected blast of February rain.

The second was the grinning, gurning face of Danny Olini.

*

Danny settled himself on the sofa and put his grubby trainers up on the cushions. He let out a long, raucous yawn, like a bored lion.

"Got anything to eat?"

Since he had arrived (twenty-three minutes ago), he had eaten all the crisps and all the apples. Before he arrived, the caravan seemed spacious. Now it felt tiny. Danny somehow took over all the space around him. His breath, smelling of cheese and onion, mingled with the sweet, muddy aroma of his trainers. He had sprayed himself with his big brother's deodorant and a heady smell of jungle chemicals filled the air.

"We're on HOLIDAY, like you," he roared. "But it's COLD. Holidays are supposed to be WARM."

"You'll need to go all the way to New Zealand if you want a warm holiday in February," supplied Merry. "Why not go there?" She smiled a falsely sweet smile. She was being, Donald decided, *nearly* mean.

He blinked at her in a purposeful manner.

Merry blinked back at him, equally purposeful.

Danny Olini didn't notice any blinking. "What a dump."

Donald had found a space on the floor, his knees around his ears like a fat spider, and Merry was wedged against the table. Mum had barricaded herself in the bathroom.

Danny Olini was the youngest of four brothers. His mum worked in a bank and his dad was an aeroplane mechanic. The family all seemed perfectly normal, apart from Danny, and Donald had speculated many times whether, as a baby, Danny had been possessed by the spirit of some mad caveman, or a gladiator, or maybe a rogue elephant.

Merry drummed her fingers on the table and looked fixedly out the window at the rain-washed car park. Donald wondered if she was having second thoughts.

"I'm having second thoughts," she said. "I don't want to be ungrateful, but a week is so long."

"I'm here for a week too," said Danny happily. "I might as well chill out with you guys. My folks won't notice I'm not with them."

Someone banged on the door.

"Danny? Are you in there?"

Mum manoeuvred herself out of the bathroom and opened the door.

Mrs Olini stood on the metal steps with her three other sons and Mr Olini.

"Hello, is Danny with you?" Mrs Olini was quite small and very smartly dressed in a skirt and jacket, like she had just come from a shift at the bank. Her black heels made an important clanking noise on the metal steps of the caravan.

"I've just finished a shift at the bank," said Mrs Olini. "We drove straight here. I forgot my suitcase." She had brown hair cut very short on her neck and coming down like curtains either side of her face. Danny's dad was a big, quiet sort of man, who tended to leave his wife to do the talking.

"Hi, Mum," said Danny from the depths of the sofa.

"Sorry about him barging in," said Mrs Olini to Mum. "He's that sort of child. Our others aren't like him at all."

"It's fine," said Mum, faking a smile.

"Sometimes I wonder if he got dropped as a baby. We're number 5678, by the way," said Mrs Olini.

"Right. Next. Door," said Mum flatly.

"I see you brought your dog with you," said Mrs Olini. (Donald's mouth fell open.)

"We haven't got a dog," said Mum.

"Hmmm," said Mrs Olini.

"We're going parachute-diving," said Danny's biggest brother (who I think is called Billy, but I'm not sure because we haven't been introduced. I may be the narrator of this story but I don't know everything).

"Sounds horrendous," said Mum.

"I know," said Mrs Olini.

Danny was already on his feet. "You guys are having the shortest conversations ever. It's like blah blah BLAH, and then someone else goes, BLAH BLAH, and then someone else says, BLAH BLAH BLAH. Are you aliens pretending to be humans?"

"Shut up, Danny," said his father in a rare intervention.

"Blah blah BLAH," said Danny. He winked at Merry. "Looks like we're going to be spending a lot of time together."

"Blah blah," said Merry, as the door slammed.

CHAPTER FiFTEEN

Danny's Secret

The Belle View swimming pool was in a large building with a metal roof like an airport terminal. There were five water slides, including the Plume of Doom. Donald had gone down twenty-seven times and his nose was still buzzing from the wash of wrong-way water. There was also a Jacuzzi, a whirlpool, a waterfall and a pretend beach.

"Isn't this AMAZING?" said Merry, splashing past on an inflatable killer whale. A shadow streaked under the water after her. Donald recognized the square head.

Danny Olini.

He watched as Danny rose from the depths and tipped Merry over.

She surfaced, spluttering and snapping.

"NOT FUNNY."

Danny looked hurt. "Just having a laugh."

Donald sensed his mother looking at him. She was sitting in the bit where the parents could drink coffee and laze around whilst keep an eye on their children.

"Having fun?" she mouthed.

Donald nodded and threw a beach ball for Bear.

Two days had passed since they'd arrived. In this time they had been to the swimming pool six times. Donald had also survived a fencing lesson with Danny and Merry and had walked over water inside a giant inflatable ball.

The vast TV screen over the coffee bar was broadcasting a news report showing epic cliff slides, where tonnes and tonnes of rock and stone and earth had plunged to the seashore. It was happening a few miles along the coast from Belle View.

Then Donald noticed a hunched figure mopping the tiles. His grey hair was pulled back into a ponytail and he wore blue overalls. Donald knew he was a Nothing because he could see plastic green ferns through him. The figure nodded at Donald, who turned his attention back to the TV screen.

FREAK HURRICANE IN DORSET

There were images of flattened hedges and an overturned ice-cream van.

"IT'S A FREAK ALL RIGHT,"
whispered a voice.

Donald steadied himself on the edge of the pool. The ghost had appeared right by his side. Close up he had heavy, pouched skin, like a very fat person who has lost lots of weight but whose skin is left like a slouchy empty bag.

"Hello," said Donald politely.

"IT'S A-COMING."
The cleaner ghost pointed his mop at the TV screen. He spoke in a singing, whispery kind of way.

"What's a-coming?" asked Donald.

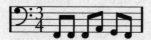

"THE BEAST OF ALL BEASTS,"
replied the cleaner in his breathy voice.

"BEAST CAN'T TELL THE DIFFERENCE BETWEEN THE LIVING AND THE DEAD."

He spoke in rhythm, but not like hip-hop.

The cleaner leaned closer to Donald and there was a whiff of disinfectant.

"HE CAN EAT US ALL."

"THAT'S NOT GOOD," said Donald, unconsciously copying the Nothing's way of speaking. He wondered if this "Beast" was the other job Mum had to deal with.

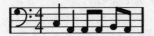

"NAME'S MO.

I WORKED HERE WHEN IT WAS JUST A CAMPSITE.

NOW IT'S LIKE VEGAS."

"How did you die?" asked Donald politely.

But Mo looked startled. "Whaaa? What did you say?"

"Never mind," said Donald. He didn't want to be the one to break the news. Mo ran off over the water, then scrunched in on himself like he was made of cling film, and was sucked into a vent at the side of the pool.

"Whatcha doing?"

Donald nearly fell in as a wet finger tapped his bare shoulder.

Danny Olini.

"You scared me," said Donald, righting himself.

"I scare everyone," said Danny. He sighed a contented sigh. "This place is brilliant. It's like being inside a happy factory." He spotted Merry. She was sitting motionless, eyes shut under a waterfall. The water poured over her head, making her hair look like it had been painted.

"I love that woman," he sighed.

Donald nearly fell in again. "You can't say that out loud!"

"Why? Don't you think she's good enough for me?"

Donald did some fast thinking. "Because you're eleven years old."

"I'll be twelve in one hundred and fifty-one days," said Danny. "Practically a man." He leaned over. "The thing is," he said confidentially, "I don't think she sees the poet in my soul."

Donald didn't like the idea of poets being in people's souls. It sounded like a bad case of haunting.

"You don't think I badgered my mum to bring us here just so I could hang out with you, did ya? Monkey bum? No, I'm here for my one true love."

"Oh shut up," said Donald, not knowing what else to say.

126

Danny tipped him into the pool.

Underwater was peaceful, but when Donald opened his eyes to see which way was up, he saw the ghost of Mo the cleaner right by his face.

"BEWARE OF THE BEAST,"
he said in a waterlogged voice.

Donald kicked, gasping, to the surface.

"Hey, No-Brain," smiled Danny from the edge. "You like you've seen a ghost."

Back in the caravan, Donald, Merry and Mum sat round the tiny table eating their dinner of fish fingers, chips and peas, trying to avoid knocking each other's knees.

"How are you enjoying your holiday?" asked Mum, a pea skin stuck to her front tooth.

"It's wonderful," said Merry. "Apart from Danny Olini."

"Epic." Donald decided not to tell Merry about Danny Olini's love for her.

A clap of thunder echoed round the sky and rumbled on and on.

Mum gripped the table and shot a look at Donald.

"Odd," she mouthed.

"Look." Merry pointed at the shelves where the cups and plates were doing a clacking tap dance.

"Earthquake?" said Mum, holding on to her dinner.

"Military manoeuvre?"

Donald remembered the noises they had heard on the first day in the car. This was the same, only louder. Much louder.

"We're in metal box in a thunderstorm." Merry swallowed. "Is this wise?"

A second rumble made the fruit bowl wobble and apples thumped to the floor. Another mighty crash made the walls shake and their peas jumped off their plates. Then there was the creak of bending metal.

THUMP!

"What on earth was that?" shrieked Mum.

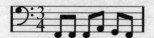

"THE BEAST OF ALL BEASTSSSS,"
muttered Donald.

Merry dashed to the door (three steps away) and fumbled with the handle.

"Hurry," said Donald. But the key was stuck.

Things were crashing and banging all around them. Donald drew back the window curtain. Outside it was not quite dark.

THUMP!

Four doors down a car was perched on the roof of a caravan.

Donald saw an airwave sweeping like a flock of birds. A tremor ran through his body. This wasn't some major weather incident. This was supernatural. It was a thousand times stronger than the mad vicar, and more oppressive and terrifying even than the supermarket ghosts. His legs felt rubbery and wobbly and wouldn't hold him up. He fell gently back on to the sofa.

Mum was looking at him, blank terror on her face. Merry had her hands over her ears.

THUMP!

Donald breathed.

"It's THEM," he croaked. "Nothings."

Merry finally managed to get the door open.

"You won't believe this."

The scene that met their eyes was unimaginable.

The air was full of swirling, whirling objects: drinks cans, crisp packets, odd shoes, flowerpots, hats, sunglasses, roof tiles and clothing danced in the air, defying gravity in some kind of unnatural wind. The children's climbing frame had been crushed into a perfect ball of red metal. The toilet block no longer had a roof and the blue-and-yellow Belle View flags hung in shreds.

They watched open-mouthed from the steps of the caravan as a dense hedge of lelandii trees toppled like dominoes, one by one.

"Look," Merry squeaked as a large shadow moved fast above them. The BELLE VIEW HOLIDAY CAMP sign curled and twisted in the air like it was made of tinfoil. It bounced off the clock tower and flew up into the dark sky and out towards the sea. The screams of the guests were caught in gusts of wind and bowled up into the sky.

Merry gripped the stair rail. There was a relentless

pressure building all around her, and it felt like her ears were going to explode. There was a thud under her feet and the whole caravan trembled.

And then, all at once, everything stopped.

"What was that?" Merry gasped. But when she turned round, she saw Donald lying unconscious in the doorway.

CHAPTER SIXTEEN

The Cliffhanger

People were going home. A line of cars and camper vans queued up the road, stuffed with hastily packed suitcases. Drivers leaned on their horns as children squabbled in the back, outraged that their holidays had been cut short. Uniformed staff were running up and down the lines, handing out forms and trying to calm tempers. The night had been alive with fire crews cutting and sawing at the wreckage. A boy had a bruised foot when a signpost landed on him and somebody's dad had a touch of concussion from a flying bench. Apart from that, everyone was OK. Even Donald, who had come round after about ten seconds and couldn't remember fainting at all, only had a bruise on his cheek.

And now he, Merry and Danny Olini leaned on the windowsill, eating biscuits and wiping away the condensation to watch.

Merry had texted her mother.

Massive hurricane. Caravans broken. Don't
worry. We R not dead.

She didn't mention it was possibly due to an epic haunting. Susie might make her come home and she didn't want to go any more. This had been the most exciting couple of days of her life.

"We didn't hear a thing," said Danny delicately peeling the rubber seal from the window. "Must have had the telly on too loud. And there's no way we're going home in the middle of the holiday." He smiled at Merry. "Now we'll have the swimming pool to ourselves. No queuing for the water slides. FAN-TAS-TICO."

Danny Olini had caused more destruction and chaos in the small caravan in thirty minutes than last night's unexplained, gargantuan event. The cushions had been kicked off the chairs; a bottle of milk had been spilled over the floor and was being slowly soaked up by a pair of Mum's knickers. There were mud-smeared footprints all over the worktops and Danny had blocked the toilet with one of his legendary giant poos.

Donald decided to tell Danny the truth.

"It wasn't a hurricane. It was an unnatural force."

"Like my farts!" laughed Danny.

Donald wondered how he could explain it without sounding crazy. "I think it was a giant ghost. There was this dead cleaner at the pool and. . ."

Danny laughed. "Donald Memphis, you are mad."

"It was! Some incredible phantom. A beast," Donald pressed on.

"Mad!"

"Ask my mum."

Danny nodded. "She's mad too."

"Ask Merry."

Danny winked at her. "She's mad in a cute way."

Merry choked on her biscuit.

"It might be dangerous. It could come back," said Donald.

"Really?" Merry frowned.

"Yes," said Donald.

"Cool," said Merry.

"I missed it the first time," said Danny. "I'm not going anywhere."

There was a tap at the door and Mrs Olini stuck her head round. She was wearing a yellow Belle View T-shirt and yellow Belle View jogging bottoms. On her head was a yellow Belle View woolly hat. She looked like a human version of the Dazzle Van.

"Danny," she said. "I'm going shopping in town for clothes for me. I cannot wear this yellow stuff a minute longer. I know you hate shopping, so can you stay with Donald?"

"Yes a way," said Danny. (He'd caught the expression off Donald too, only he'd twisted it round because he was Danny Olini.)

Mum appeared from the bathroom. "Going home?" she asked hopefully.

"The storm's over," replied Mrs Olini. "It will be easier here with less people around." She shot a tired look at Danny.

"We're about to go for a family walk," said Mum.

Mothers have a secret language. "*We're about to go for a family walk*" means "*Get your awful pesky kid out of my hair*". Mrs Olini, being a mother, understood this. But she hoped that the Higher Rule of Mothers would prevail. This rule meant whichever mother was most desperate got to dump her kid on the other.

"Fantastico!" said Danny. "I love walks. Can I come? Please. Please. Please?"

"Shopping brings out the worst in him," said Mrs Olini. "The last time I took him, they had to call out the police dogs."

"Um," said Mum.

The Higher Rule of Mothers was coming into play.

Mrs Olini adjusted her yellow T-shirt.

It was a stand-off.

Mum looked pained.

"Your husband. . .?" she suggested.

"We forgot his suitcase too," said Mrs Olini.

"I promise I'll be good, Mrs Memphis," said Danny, sensing weakness.

"Um," said Mum, desperately flailing for an excuse.

"What could possibly go wrong?" said Danny.

*

TWENTY MINUTES LATER.

"What's that smell?" asked Mum as she drove up a cliff road. Danny, who was sitting in the front passenger seat, laughed sheepishly.

"Probably me, I had beans for breakfast."

"No, it smells like a dog."

In the back seat, Donald tickled Bear's neck.

"Do you like dogs, Mrs M?" asked Merry innocently.

"No. They're noisy and too needy. A bit like husbands." Mum spoke like she thought no one could hear her. She turned off the road into a deserted clifftop car park.

As everyone climbed out of the car, Donald noticed that Bear stayed well away from Mum.

"Don't worry," he whispered. "She won't see you unless you get really close."

Bear wagged his tail and trotted off to investigate some rabbity-looking bushes.

The car park was a few hundred yards from the edge of a high cliff. The wind was blowing cold and the sea far below was flecked with foam.

"This is the Jurassic Coast," Mum shouted into the wind. "It's world famous for its fossil beaches." The wind plastered her scarf on to her head and her long skirt blew out behind her.

A long line of police tape was strung one hundred metres back from the edge of the cliff.

"Feel that wild energy," shouted Mum, standing in a star shape.

Donald shot an embarrassed look at Merry, but she

grinned. She came from an eccentric family and was used to adults behaving oddly. Danny Olini, however, took a step away from Mum and made a "she's crazy"* face.

Donald could understand why Mum liked it up here. It felt clean and fresh, and, apart from the ghost of an overweight puffin, he could see no Nothings. It made him want to run about like a mad horse.†

Faint sunshine pressed through the clouds, making Merry's eyes sparkle and turning the sea silver.

"Why are we here?" Danny asked Mum, his hands buried deep in his deep pockets.

"To see the spectacle of cliff erosion," she replied.

All along the coast they saw mountains of brown and grey rubble and stone heaped on the beach.

"What caused that?" asked Donald.

"Bad weather, strong winds . . . unexplained hurricanes," said Merry, looking sideways at him.

Donald turned to Mum. "Mum? Is this part of, you know, IT?"

"Maybe," said Mum. She looked deep into his eyes. "Do you sense anything?"

Donald shifted uneasily from foot to foot. "Dunno," he said.

---

* Why don't you try making a "she's crazy" face? Great! Go and look at yourself in the mirror. You can use this face any time your mother (or father) suggests something preposterous, like going to bed or doing your homework.
† You could also try this.

Mum looked fleetingly disappointed, then did another star jump.

"I'm hungry," announced Danny Olini.

"Don't go under the police tape, Danny," Mum called in a trying-not-to-be-fussy parent voice, as Danny ducked under and scampered towards the cliff edge.

"Just seeing how dangerous it is," he said, looking back with a knowing grin.

"Come back, please." Mum injected serious notes into her voice.*

Now Danny was only fifty metres away from the crumbling cliff edge.

"DANNY," shrieked Mum, going up to top E. "It's dangerous. Come back."

"Half a tick," shouted Danny, speeding up. "Don't fret, lady."

Donald and Merry swapped anguished glances. Even Bear looked concerned.

"Stay here." Mum ducked under the police lines. She scuttled after Danny, her long skirt getting tangled in the tussocky grass.

"Don't touch him," Donald shouted. "He'll go nuts."

If anyone tried to steer Danny Olini, he lashed out. Teachers at school had learned to mind-control him with words, threats and bribery instead of brute force.

"Mum, think of him as a level ten!" shouted Donald. "Don't go any closer!"

---

* The notes were D and C.

137

"I can't let him fall off the cliff," snapped Mum, hitching up her skirt and jumping over a rock. "Come here, Danny. This is NAUGHTY." She lunged for him but he only increased his speed, his face twisting and changing into a mad-Dan face.

"He's turning crazy," said Merry, recognizing the signs. "There's no Safe Space out here."

"Danny, come back or I'll tell Merry what you told me," yelled Donald.

But Danny wasn't listening to anyone.

"Tell me what?" asked Merry.

"You're TOO CLOSE TO THE EDGE," shrieked Mum, speeding up.

Donald had an awful vision of his mother and Danny struggling on the cliff edge, slipping and plummeting to the sea rocks below.

"MUM," he screamed. "He'll take you with him." He had never seen his mum move so fast. She was running as fast as a kid! They watched as she flung out one blue-nailed hand and grabbed Danny.

"He's gonna blow!" Merry had her hands over her eyes.

And when Mum's wind-chilled fingers clutched Danny's collar, he flinched and exploded outwards, arms lashing and feet kicking.

"Mum!" screamed Donald. He bent under the tape and ran to the struggling pair, who were like eggs rolling on the edge of a table.

But Danny had seen the drop. In alarm, he lost his

balance and swayed backwards, like magnets were pulling him down. Donald pelted towards them. But it was too late. They seemed to be dancing off the side into the sky.

"MUM!"

CHAPTER SEVENTEEN

Bear

A charge pushed past Donald towards the cliff. Then a black cloud pounced on Mum and Danny and extracted them out of the air. The cloud formed the figure of a large black dog as it shouldered the pair away from the edge.

Bear!

The dog grasped Danny's collar in his teeth and yanked the boy behind the police tape. Danny's arms and legs dragged along the ground and his head slumped forward.

Mum scuttled behind. "Good boy!" she panted. "Good, good, GOOD boy."

"I think your mum has changed her mind about dogs," observed Merry shakily.

Donald couldn't say anything. If it hadn't been for Bear, his mother and Danny might be dead.

Mum couldn't stop babbling.

"What a dog. WHAT a dog," and she scratched his back in the way he exactly liked.

Seeing his mum there, safe, with her hair all crazy and her necklaces flashing in the sunlight, made Donald throw his arms around her.

"But how come you can see him now when you didn't before?" he mumbled.

"I know Bear," said Mum, breathless. "It's a long story and I haven't got the oxygen for it now. Can we go?"

They strapped a stunned Danny into the back seat and with Bear curled up in the boot, drove slowly down to the nearest town, which was called Lyme Regis.

In The Fossil Shack, a beachside café, after they'd polished off several rounds of toast and scrambled eggs, Mum explained about Bear, her cold hands curled around a hot chocolate.

"He's our family dog," she said. "Though he's been dead for decades."

"But he's not in any photos or stories," said Donald.

"Yes he is, I just haven't showed you." Mum settled in her chair.

"When my great-granny was a girl, she had a dog, called Bear. He was a cross between a Great Dane and an Irish wolfhound. He was the biggest dog anyone had ever seen. When my great-granny was three years old, she fell into a pond. Bear pulled her out and saved her life. One day he vanished. Everyone assumed he had been stolen. The family was heartbroken. But twenty years later, Great-Granny was crossing the road and didn't see the car that came whizzing round the corner. Granny fainted, but the driver later swore a huge black dog appeared from nowhere and carried her to safety."

Mum took a sip of chocolate, her bracelets clinking.

"I only saw him once, and that was at my great-grandmother's funeral. He was sitting in the churchyard. Everyone said that his ghost would die along with Granny, but many, many years later, Uncle John was out surfing and got caught in a rip tide. He thought he was going to drown as the water kept turning him over and over. He said he saw a huge black shape come for him. He was found on the beach with teeth marks in his wetsuit. Everyone said it was Bear. And the funny thing was, John said he could have sworn the dog had been following him for a few weeks before the incident."

"Spooky," said Merry.

"Why didn't you tell me about him?" asked Donald, dunking marshmallows in his hot chocolate.

"He only appears when family members are in great danger. . ." Mum's voice trailed off.

"But does this mean Bear will go away, now he's saved you?" Donald felt around under the table and was reassured to find Bear lying by his feet.

"I hope so," said Mum. "Because if he stays around, it means one of us is still in deadly danger."

"But Bear will save us," said Donald confidently.

His mother took a long breath. "Some forces are stronger than others."

"Do you mean the Hurricane Beast Thing? Is Bear still here because of that?" asked Donald. "Is it going to come back?"

"I think so," said Mum quietly.

Bear grumbled under the table and Donald rubbed his back with his foot.

"Would Bear eat my sausage?" asked Merry, trying to lighten the mood. "Will I see it all mashed up in the air once he's swallowed it?"

"Try," said Donald, so Merry slipped her sausage under the table. Bear ate it in less than a second and then it vanished.

"How does that work?" asked Merry. "Where has it gone? How can something that isn't really here make something solid vanish?"

"There's an awful lot we don't know about the spiritual world," said Mum.

The café woman brought them over another round of hot chocolates and Donald studied the green-painted wooden walls. They were covered with posters advertising old boats for sale, fishing trips and fossil-hunting expeditions.

He nudged Mum and pointed to a sign about an event that happened two nights ago.

ESTELLA GREY
GIFTED AND CERTIFIED MEDIUM
AND CLAIRVOYANT
APPEARING AT THE GRAND HOTEL
TICKETS £12

"Is that Estella, Estella?" asked Donald.

"Oh yes," said Mum. "She loves doing the stage shows. I expect to hear from her soon. After all, she's the reason we're here."

Donald read the next poster.

MUSEUM BREAK-IN

Any information, no matter how small, regarding
the museum break-in at Lyme Regis last month
should be reported to the police.
Many valuable fossils were stolen.
No arrests have been made.

"Who'd want to steal a load of old bones?" remarked Donald.

"Him?" suggested Merry, pointing to a gold poster.

WILF TOWNLEY
CELEBRITY TV PALAEONTOLOGIST
WILL IDENTIFY YOUR FOSSILS
FOR SMALL FEE
AUTOGRAPHS WELCOME

There was a big photograph of a tousled blond man in a red jumper. He looked like a grown-up pop singer.

"What's a palay . . . paleee . . . paleee . . . on . . . toll . . . lo . . . gist?" asked Donald. What a foul and difficult word. It was like a sum; you had to add it up to make it work.

144

"Palaeontologist – someone who studies fossils," said Merry. "The rocks here are full of them."

"How can you be a celebrity of fossils?" asked Donald.

"You can be a celebrity of anything if you have the right haircut," said Merry.

"No one's giving me a haircut." Danny Olini, slumped in a comfy chair by the window, had opened his eyes. These were the first words he had spoken since he had fallen and then unfallen off the cliff.

"Can you remember anything?" asked Merry, turning away from the posters.

"Course I can," frowned Danny. "I can remember my name, my birthday and where my brother hides his sweetie stash."

"Do you remember anything about the cliff?" said Merry. "Did you see Bear?"

"What bear?" Danny frowned.

"Can't you see him now?" persisted Merry. "He's sniffing your hand."

Danny stretched and sat up, an unusually serious expression on his face.

"No," he said firmly. "Merry, you've been hanging out with these ghostbusters too long. There's no such things as ghosts. Mum says Mrs Memphis makes it all up to earn a living."

"Thank you, Danny," said Mum stiffly.

"I remember looking at the view; then Mrs Memphis came along and she pushed me over. Then I can't remember anything."

"I DID NOT push you over," said Mum, flaring up. "I asked you to come back from the edge and you didn't listen. You put us both in grave danger."

"Grave danger," mumbled Donald. "Danger of the Grave."

"Sorry about that." Danny Olini suddenly smiled. "Tell you what, Mrs M. You don't mention that I didn't listen to you, and I won't mention how you pushed me. Deal?"

He was becoming more like himself every minute.

Mum was cross. Donald could tell by her white knuckles and the fact that her lips had disappeared into her mouth.

"I shan't be taking you out again. Not until you learn to behave yourself."

"Well, I've learned," said Danny, flashing her a smile. "Don't mess with Mrs M or she'll try to kill you."

CHAPTER EIGHTEEN

The Gathering of "The Believers"

Donald lay in bed in the depths of the night, listening to branches behind the caravan scrape over the metal walls. He missed his dad. He missed him so much it gave him a tight feeling in his chest. What was Dad doing? Was he even in his house, or did he appear only when Donald came? Donald wanted to ask him about the supernatural hurricane. There was nothing about it he recognized. No smells or feelings. He only knew it was a mighty force, and it was funny to say, but it was a dead feeling. Like he was dealing with the ghost of a rock.

Donald found himself getting confused, and then it was suddenly* morning and everything seemed all right again.

Who knows?

The best thing about morning is, of course, breakfast, and this particular holiday breakfast consisted of porridge with raspberries, strawberries and a fat swirl of chocolate sauce.

Mum's phone rang. She checked the number on the screen, gave the children a sneaky glance and retreated to her bedroom.

Donald leaned back and folded his arms. "She only makes telephone calls private when they're about dodgy hauntings."

"Which means this call is likely to be about our mad haunting," said Merry.

"Which means we should listen," said Donald.

Merry made a face. "Eavesdropping is wrong."

"Yes," said Donald. "But we might be in danger. If a bit of eavesdropping saves our lives, then I think it's OK."

They prepared to listen but the walls were thin, and Mum's whispering voice was louder than her talking voice, so the children didn't have to do anything more scandalous than sit quietly.

"*Estella, I'm really not sure. . .*" whispered Mum, as loud as a windstorm in a metal pipe.

"Estella invited Mum here," explained Donald. "She's like the queen of mediums. She has a club called The Believers. When you join you can put a badge on your website, so everyone knows you really can see ghosts and

---

* Of course it wasn't "suddenly" morning. Nine dark hours had passed. Unless, of course, time doesn't exist when you are asleep. In which case, it really WAS "suddenly".

you're not making it up. They have loads of different levels. Estella is at the top. She's supposed to be really talented. She's got a gold badge. No one gets gold badges."

"What level is April?" asked Merry, interested.

"Amazingly, she's got a silver," said Donald, feeling his face burn. He didn't know how she'd got that far.

"She's much better than you think," said Merry. "My mum says, apart from you, she's the most talented medium she's ever met."

"But one minute she sees everything and the next, it's like she's gone blind," said Donald. He'd never admitted this to anyone before. "I never know what ghosts she sees and what she doesn't."

"You see more ghosts than anyone," said Merry. "Don't expect her to be as good as you. Don't expect anyone to be as good as you."

"*What? All of us?*" Mum was no longer whispering.

Her voice rose an octave, which is quite impressive when you are whispering. Reader. Yes, you. Try it now. Whisper something, then go eight notes up and whisper it again.

Something !!!!
Something.
Something.
Something.
Something.
Something.
Something.
Start Here. Something.

How was that? Squeaky?

Anyway. Back to Mum's strictly private phone conversation.

"*You all want to come here?*"

"Here here?" Donald looked round the thin metal walls of the caravan. What was his mother up to?

"*The poor thing will be scared away.*"

"No it won't," murmured Donald. He shivered. When he thought about IT, he saw images of burning cauldrons, the inside of volcanos, and fiery rivers like the ones in Mount Doom in *The Lord of the Rings*.

The door to Mum's room burst open. Her cheeks were flushed and she fanned herself with her hands.

"EVERYONE is coming here," she said, not secretly at all. "Estella says this is a case for a mass event. We need every registered medium and mystic in the country to combat this force."

Donald's mouth fell open. Merry gently nudged it shut.

"How many is everyone?" Merry asked.

"Ooh, about ten thousand," said Mum. "And they'll all be here by teatime."

Of course, in the end there weren't ten thousand. As the mediums gathered in the car park at five p.m., Donald counted forty-three.

There were men, woman, old and young. Donald noticed one girl with short blonde hair and purple trousers. She couldn't have been more than fifteen. She caught Donald staring and deliberately turned her back.

"That's Claire Voyant," said Mum, who had come over all shy and hadn't yet set foot outside the caravan. "She's one of the most gifted young psychics I know."

"Don't worry, I bet she's not as talented as you," Merry whispered to Donald.

"Oh, she's not!" said Mum. "Everyone knows Donald is the best in the land."

Donald glowed. The Best in the Land! Crikey. She'd never said that before.

He noticed a tall, broad man with a flowing red beard and an impressive belly, as big and round as a spacehopper. He was dressed in a black suit and carried a rainbow-striped umbrella.

"Old Joe," said Mum. "He's also very talented."

A trio of women were hugging and shrieking, one dressed entirely in green, one in blue and the other in red. They all had long sleek hair and were aged about forty.

"The Sardonique Sisters," said Mum. "They work very powerfully as a trio, harnessing all their strengths. Oh look, Estella Grey has arrived. I suppose I ought to go out and meet her." She did not move.

"You're scared of her," said Donald.

"No, I'm not. We just have some complicated history," sighed Mum.

"Why did you come, then?" asked Donald.

"Because I was worried about this THING, whatever it is. It's so unusual."

The children watched as Mum timidly threaded through

151

the crowd to a tall woman with brown curly hair cut into a stylish bob. She had laugh lines and frown lines etched into her face.

"She's almost pretty, in a scary kind of way," remarked Merry.

Donald had met Estella several times. She reminded him of a certain type of schoolteacher. One who never panicked or flapped, and had the sort of voice that people listened to.

They watched as Mum awkwardly tapped Estella on the shoulder. Donald had noticed that when Mum felt shy, she, like him, grew tongue-tied and clumsy. He saw a gleam pass over Estella's face and she stared in his direction when Mum pointed out their caravan.

Donald shuddered.

Twenty minutes later and the crowd started moving.

"Where are they all going?" asked Merry.

"Somewhere they won't be overheard," said Donald. "Somewhere neutral where they can channel their powers. Somewhere soulless, and lacking deep magic. Somewhere no one will notice a crowd of spiritualists and druids and witches."

"What are they going to do?" Merry watched them with great interest.

Donald had been wondering this too. Mum hadn't given him any information, though she had taken a towel with her.

"I think they're going to do a mass séance. Like a big group ghost hunt to find the thing that's causing all these hurricanes," he said. "It's not what I'd do. I'd just try and talk to it."

"If they don't stop now they'll end up in the swimming pool," remarked Merry.

The group ended up in the swimming pool.

Donald and Merry sat sipping milkshakes through straws as one by one, the newcomers lowered themselves into the pool.

"I never thought I would see forty-three ghost hunters in their swimsuits," said Merry. "How I am experiencing life."

"Donald. At last." Estella, wrapped in a rose-pink towel and wagging her head from side to side, put a hand on his shoulder. "What is disturbing our peace?"

Donald shrugged. His tongue had turned into porridge in his mouth. Estella always seemed so important. He wanted to impress her with his foresight and perception. To make her see the true depths of his abilities with grown-up-sounding sentences and lots of long words.

"Dunno," he said, which was at least true.

"That's odd, you usually do know." Estella had a soft voice with metal core. It made Donald think of a sword wrapped in a duvet. Estella regarded Merry, who rapidly removed the straw from her nose.

"And you too have the Gift. It grows stronger as you stay with Donald."

"Um, not really. . ."

Estella turned back to Donald. "I am greatly concerned

that you do not know what this is. You. So powerful, and yet it is out of even your reach."

"You don't know what the mega-mass is either?" asked Merry. "That's pretty sick."

"Interesting phrase, mega-mass," murmured Estella.

The buzz of the tannoy rang out over the water and a lively pop song blasted out of the speakers.

"I must go," said Estella. "Be alert to everything." She strode off to the side of the pool and shrugged off her towel to reveal a pink-and-black stretchy thing that went all the way down to her ankles.

"I'm so rubbish," sighed Donald. "I get star-struck with people who aren't even stars."

"That's because you think everyone is special and important because you're a nice person," said Merry. Donald stared at her and she went red.

"Thanks," said Donald. He swallowed. "You're a nice person too, mostly."

"So does that make us official friends?" asked Merry. "Even at school?"

"I guess," said Donald. "But not, like, boyfriend and girlfriend," he added hurriedly.

"No a way," replied Merry. She pointed. "Oh, do look now!"

Estella had started doing star jumps on the edge of the pool.

"And let's go," she shouted, raising her arms. "One, two, three."

Everyone copied her, spinning in the pool as Estella

twirled. Donald gripped the table. This was way out of his comfort zone. Stay alert? He could hardly bear to look.

"This isn't a mass séance." Merry's straw was stuck to her lip. "This is aqua aerobics."

"The perfect camouflage," said Donald.

CHAPTER NiNETEEN

Whirlpool

Have you ever watched an aqua aerobics session? No? Taken part in one?

For those of you who have never experienced this experience, you get a group of people, bung them in a swimming pool, and get them to do dance moves to banging pop music.

Forty-four people bouncing and swaying create a lot of currents. Not the currants you get in cakes. As the mediums danced, the swimming pool was awash with small tides and waves, pulling them this way and that. Estella barked at them to join hands and they moved slowly round in a circle, creating a gentle whirlpool. A skinny old man tripped and went underwater and had to be hauled to the surface.

"FASTER," shrieked Estella. "YOU'RE TOO SLOW."

"She's really bossy," observed Merry. "Why are they all doing what she says? Why doesn't someone say, No, you bossy old bag, who put you in charge anyway?"

"She's powerful," said Donald. "And she's got a plan."

"Dreadful music," shuddered Merry. "This is like an old person's disco."

Donald explained the music was a disguise. Mediums liked to keep a low profile.

"They're channelling," said Donald, finishing off his milkshake. From his vantage point he could see a blue swirl in the fuggy, muggy air above the swimmers. Mum had her eyes tightly shut, and held hands with Old Joe on one side (in tartan trunks) and the Claire Voyant girl on the other (in purple).

Donald saw Mo, the ghost cleaner, standing on the side and wondered if any of the mediums had sensed him.

He caught Estella's eye and she nodded at him, then at Mo. At least she'd seen him.

"That is really something," breathed Merry, looking at the whirling, swirling cloud as it grew denser and formed into a vortex.

A ghost gull piled through the roof and glided into the cloud. Immediately Old Joe, the ginger-bearded man, started squawking like someone was robbing his nest. Then Mo dived off the side right into the whirlpool, holding his mop like a lightsabre.

"Listen," said Merry, as a low roar, like the ticking of a giant engine, emanated from the cloud.

"KEEP HOLDING HANDS," Estella commanded. "If something BIG comes along, we'll need all our energy to hold it."

The lifeguard, a young man of about eighteen in red shorts, strolled out of a door and climbed into his high chair. He watched the group with great curiosity. He could not see the cloud.

"One, two, three, WORK IT!" called Estella. "Lift those legs!"

The lifeguard looked away.

Donald and Merry watched as a striped ghost cat ("Aw," said Merry), a dead elderly holidaymaker in a flowery sundress and the spirit of the town mayor all slipped into the whirlwind.

The circle of mediums began cackling and meowing, screeching and coughing.

"What are they trying to do?" asked Merry.

"They're opening their minds to attract the ghosts in the area. If they combine thoughts, they become like one BIG powerful magnet medium. They hope this will draw in IT, whatever IT is."

"I sort of see," said Merry. "But why do they want to make IT come?"

Donald shook his head. "Maybe they want to see what they're dealing with."

"But what if it pulverizes the place?" said Merry. "People might get hurt."

"There's not many people left," said Donald. "They've all gone home."

"Except them." Merry pointed as a large family group carrying big pink inflatables and snorkels entered the fun pool.

The Olini family.

"Nothing can hurt them," said Donald. "They're indestructible."

Merry and Donald sank lower in their seats.

The lifeguard twitched in his chair as the circle of mediums yelped like mad meerkats and more and more ghosts slid into the cloud.

Donald watched behind his fingers. The circle was attracting the ghosts, but it was embarrassing to watch lots of oldish people jigging around in their swimsuits.

The lifeguard climbed down his ladder and headed to the mediums' pool.

"It's a new form of exercise called Chase Out Your Demons! It's so good for the lungs! Come and try it!" cried Estella.

"Er, no thanks," said the lifeguard.

Donald was transfixed. Would IT come?

There was a rumble, like thunder, overhead.

"It's coming," said Merry nervously.

Terror began to form in Donald's stomach like a bad pie.

The noise grew louder, sounding like the groan of a low-flying heavy plane.

Estella had noticed too. She stopped dancing.

The rumbling deepened and the water shivered.

Donald felt a whine in his ears, starting quietly then growing in intensity.

"Get out," he said suddenly to Merry. "NOW." But Merry had her hands clamped over her ears.

Some of the mediums had stopped moving.

"DON'T BREAK THE CIRCLE," yelled Estella. "It will stop everything."

Mum broke the circle. It did not stop everything.

"Darlings, I think you should leave. I can sense a. . ."

"We should ALL leave," Donald shouted, getting to his feet.

"This is INCREDIBLE," Estella shouted ecstatically. "NOBODY LEAVE."

"You must STOP," shouted Donald, climbing over the barrier and standing on the edge of the pool.

The lifeguard blew his whistle.

"No shoes on the poolside," he ordered, oblivious of the pressure building around him.

Donald's head felt like it was being forced on to his chest.

"Let's get YOU out of here," said Merry, taking his arm.

"I'm not leaving Mum in here," gasped Donald.

"You've gone white," said Merry. "Like you've been dipped in moon dust."

The noise grew even louder.

"Are you sure this thing is dead?" asked Merry. "Could it be a massive alien?"

"No such thing," panted Donald. He felt a nerve in his throat twitching. He felt something wet on his upper lip and when he put a finger there, it came away with blood.

"Nosebleed," said Merry.

"It's the pressure," said Donald. The air molecules around them seemed to be doing somersaults. It was like the air was *stretching*.

Old Joe let out a thin cry, like a cat seeing his mean second cousin.

"Look," gasped Merry.

The pool water had begun to swirl in the other direction. Then they heard It.

THUMP!

It shook the tables in the café. Everyone went quiet. Then another THUMP, much louder, like a tree landing. Another **THUMP** and the glass in the windows cracked.

"OUT," howled Donald through his dry throat. "OUT, OUT. MUM!"

Mum waded to the side, but the others stood transfixed. Estella was motionless, an expression of rapture on her face.

"We're in trouble," gasped Donald as the roof started to shake.

"Oh no." Merry pointed as one of the older mediums keeled over in the water. Everyone waded to help, but then another woman passed out.

The lifeguard blew his whistle, and fell off his chair as the ground shook. Donald rushed to help Mum whilst trying to block out the pounding in his head.

Medium after medium was fainting in the pool as the roof joints creaked and bent. IT was above them and was about to come in.

It was too late.

Donald hauled Mum out, put his hands over his head and waited for the roof to tear open.

CHAPTER TWENTY

Danny Olini
Saves The Day

The roaring and pounding abruptly stopped. There was a shrill keening and red lights flashed on the walls.

"IT'S GONE AWAY," shrieked Merry.

The lifeguard dived into the water and hauled a limp medium to the surface.

Apart from Mum and Estella, all the swimmers had fainted. Every. Single. One. Merry ran to the pool, jumped in and grabbed a limp Sardonique sister.

Donald forced his wobbly legs to work as he kicked off his shoes and followed suit, turning an unconscious Old Joe the right way up. Putting a rubber ring under his head, he left him to float and went to rescue someone else.

Mum and Estella joined in, helping the lifeguard fish out the motionless mediums. There was an almighty splash as the Olini family jumped in to continue the rescue. Danny Olini tugged a short man in spotty trunks to the side, then turned back and picked the green Sardonique sister off the bottom of the pool.

"Is she breathing?" asked Donald anxiously.

To his relief, she hit out and snorted.

"I was just looking for my ring," she snapped. "It's silver-plated."

A fireman burst through the door, shouting.

"Where's the fire?"

More firemen arrived. Donald noticed his mother pause for a split second to gawk as a team of six beefy men stripped to their boxer shorts and dived into the pool.

Along the sides of the pool, mediums were beginning to sit up, hacking and coughing and banging their chests.

"I set off the fire alarm," Danny Olini whispered in Donald's ear. "I thought it would be funny. I never thought the fire brigade would turn up to a fire in a swimming pool."

Donald spied the young girl medium, Claire Voyant, floating face down near the side. Quickly he splashed over. She was floating just below the surface, very peaceful, with her arms outstretched and her eyes closed. Donald pulled her up into the air.

Something was wrong.

"Help!" shouted Donald. "I don't think she's breathing."

Within seconds, one of the fire team was there. He checked Claire's pulse, and as Donald helped hold her, he blew air into her nose and mouth whilst she was still half in the water.

Donald waited, even more terrified now than he had been when IT was about to come through the roof. He should have got them all out. Why did he just sit there and let them call IT? This was all his fault.

Claire Voyant gagged. Donald felt tears of relief prickle his eyes. She hadn't drowned! She coughed horribly but the colour quickly returned to her face. She looked directly at Donald as she was carried out of the water.

Eventually, all the mediums were retrieved. One or two of them were retching and three of them, like Donald, had nosebleeds, but no one had drowned.

As Donald climbed out of the pool, Mum swooped on him.

"Thank goodness you're OK."

Donald untangled himself.

"It was the fire alarm that scared IT off," said Mum. "Estella agrees. If it hadn't gone off, the Thing would have brought the roof down." She looked at her son sideways.

"Any more of a clue what IT might be?" A couple of mediums nearby stopped coughing and listened.

Donald sat in a chair in his soaking jeans. He shut his eyes and tried to think what to say. But the sentences didn't come. All he had were words like *dead* and *rock* and *giant*. Words like *wild* and *powerful* and *crushing*. Words like *hungry, angry* and *merciless*.

Estella, wrapped in her pink fluffy towel, pressed a notepad and pen in his hands. "If you can't say it, draw it."

So, shutting out the coughs and complaints echoing round the walls, Donald drew.

"It's an ice cream," said Danny Olini.

"A tree?" suggested Merry.

"Donald, is it a hurricane?" asked Estella.

A crowd gathered.

"A caterpillar?" suggested the chief fireman, water dribbling down his manly chest.

"What a good guess!" squeaked Mum, and blushed when Donald gave her A Look.

"I saw feathers," came a quiet voice. Claire Voyant was lying on a pool lounger nearby.

Everyone looked at her.

Everyone looked back at Donald.

"It's a bit like a Christmas tree," gabbled Mum. "I do love Christmas. Lot of work, mind you."

Donald pushed the paper away. This wasn't helping.

Old Joe addressed Estella. "When we repeat this experiment, it should take place outdoors, where nothing can fall on us."

Donald thought they were all crazy. This thing was too powerful and dangerous for all of them.

No one could deal with IT.

Especially not him.

Mum had gone to bed early with the beginnings of a sore throat. Merry and Donald sat at the table, eating baked beans.

"Why don't we just ask a ghost?" said Merry, skewering

a bean and holding it aloft. "That cleaning bloke at the pool. Wouldn't he know what IT is?"

Donald had thought of this. But there was a problem.

It had been a strange and quiet afternoon for Donald. Everywhere he looked, there were no ghouls, no spirits, no ghostly birds, no old mouldering ladies or festering men. The world was as clean and new as if nothing had ever died.

Donald felt dizzy with it. There was so much space. "Have you seen any ghosts recently?" he said.

"I saw lots this morning in the swimming pool," said Merry. "They were all going into the vortex."

"So they have either all been cleansed, or they are annoyed or frightened," said Donald. "Either way, there's none about. Not even a ghost slug!"

All of the mediums had left, but Mum said some Estella's close friends were staying nearby.

Merry looked under the table. Then, with a worried glance at Donald, she lifted the curtain and peered out of the window into the darkness.

"Has Bear gone too?" she asked.

"I've not seen him," Donald said, and swallowed.

"He's survived death for decades," said Merry. "He'll be back."

"I hope so," said Donald. "He might be a bad omen but he's a good dog."

They were quiet.

"I don't know what to do," admitted Donald. "I can usually sort these things out with a bit of a chat. But this is too much."

They both jumped when there was a bang on the window.

"Let me in," said a gruff voice. "I've found your IT."

It was Danny Olini.

Now he sat on the floor, eating baked beans. His family had gone to the cinema in Dorchester, but he had been left behind because he had given his smallest big brother his bogey collection. (He'd put them on his pillow.) He was grounded and told to stay in the caravan and watch cartoons.

"So I went for a stroll to the sea," said Danny. "It seemed like a nice day for it."

"It's evening and it's been dark for four hours," said Donald.

"You have to come with me," said Danny. "I can't explain it."

"But it's night-time," protested Donald.

"Perfect," said Danny. "Where's the old lady?"

"In bed, asleep," said Merry, who had just checked.

"So let's go."

Donald, who had plenty of experience of sneaking out, was already putting on his shoes. But Merry hesitated.

"We should leave a note in case April wakes."

"Say you're with me," said Danny. "That'll put her mind at ease."

CHAPTER TWENTY-ONE

Weird Winds

As the children trudged up the hill, the lights of the caravan park faded into an orange gloom. On one side was the cliff and below that, the quiet sea. To their right were dark fields.

"Why don't you just tell us what you found instead of dragging us out here?" Merry was ratty because her feet were wet and she wanted to go to bed and read her book.

"You won't believe me unless you see it with your own eyes," replied Danny.

Ten minutes later they were walking through a wide flattish field.

"Nearly there," said Danny.

"What were you doing out here, anyway?" asked Merry.

"Remember how you went crazy on the school sponsored walk and refused to get out of the tree until Mrs Higgins gave you her Kit Kat?"

"I was young and foolish," said Danny.

"It was only five months ago," said Merry.

A small prickly bush caught Donald's boot and he stumbled. "What is this stuff? It's everywhere."

"Baby Christmas trees. This is a Christmas tree farm."

A little further on, the trees were knee-high, in serried ranks. The children filed through them, following Danny, who was singing a jaunty marching tune.

"This is like my worst nightmare," announced Merry brightly, "following him –" she pointed her torch at Danny "– into a dark forest."

"You've hurt my feelings," said Danny cheerfully.

"You have feelings?" asked Merry.

"Course," said Danny. "Feelings are what you get before lunch."

The one of trees came to an abrupt end and the children stepped into a wide, scrubby clearing.

Donald froze. "What's that?"

A tangled heap of metal, as big as a bus, gleamed dully in the moonlight. With his torch, Donald picked out a twisted climbing frame, a crushed car and twists and twists of wire fencing. The metal was shaped and bent into a circular shape.

"It's the ITs," said Danny.

Donald stepped closer.

"At first I thought it was just a pile of scrap," said Danny.

"But look." He shot off over the clearing and clambered up the heap.

"What are you waiting for?"

Donald scaled an upended park bench and hauled himself over a broken fridge. There was a rough ledge running round the top. He found himself a foothold on a bent garden spade and peered over.

The centre of the sculpture was hollowed out, like a bowl.

Danny put his leg over the side and lowered himself to the base.

"It's bizarre," said Merry. "How do you know it is connected to IT?"

"That," said Danny and shone his torch.

They saw a twisted sign bent almost over on itself, forming the base of the bowl.

BELLE VIEW HOLIDAY PARK

"But you don't believe in ghosts or phantoms or IT," said Merry.

"IT is a freak hurricane," said Danny. "Picking stuff up, spinning it around, and dumping it here. Weird winds."

Donald ran his hands over the corroded and mangled structure.

"It's nature's sculpture," said Danny, looking at Merry, obviously hoping she'd be impressed.

"It's not nature's sculpture," said Donald, slowly. "It's a nest."

He felt sick.

"You're giving me the creeps!" said Danny.

Donald blinked. "I've got plenty of those."

"That's a heck of a nest," said Merry brightly.

"It's a heck of an IT," said Donald.

"A giant ghost bird that makes a nest on the ground," mused Merry.

The walls of the nest were maybe eight feet high. Donald thought of a large bird – it must be too big to fly – stalking over the ground. A bird that would have lived around these parts years ago.

The wires in the nest jangled and hummed.

"What was that?" asked Merry nervously.

THUMP!

"Let's go," urged Donald.

THUMP! THUMP!

Donald grabbed Merry's hand and pulled her up the side of the bowl, scratching his wrist on a fence post. He paused on top of the nest. The silver sea shimmered in the distance; the dark land mass bulged behind him.

The tops of the Christmas trees began to sway.

"It's coming back," yelled Merry. "Get out of there, you idiot."

Danny was still inside the nest. "I'm not scared."

"Please, Danny," said Merry.

"Are you worried about me?" Danny began to climb at last.

Donald felt the now familiar pressure bear down on him and his skin crawled. He jumped the last few feet and landed badly. The earth beneath his knees shuddered. "RUN!" he yelped.

The three tore over the uneven ground to the edge of the clearing and plunged into the cover of the trees just as a mighty shadow passed over them. Donald looked into the sky and a low long groan escaped from his throat as he fell backwards on his bum, his elbows digging into the mud.

A deep, chilling roar filled the night as a colossal creature pounded through the clearing. Twenty feet high, it had two sturdy legs and an enormous long body. Its tail lashed out.

"Impossible," whispered Donald.

The head cocked and turned, like a terrible fanged bird with cold, reptilian eyes.

"*Dinosaur*," squeaked Merry.

CHAPTER TWENTY-TWO

The Impossible

The thing stalked the clearing, moonlight glinting on deadly teeth. It lowered its monstrous head and roared, a deep, bone-trembling sound. Light-headed with terror, Donald could do nothing but stare. He had never seen a ghost of a prehistoric animal. Spirits couldn't stick around that long. Dinosaurs were so dead, they had turned to rocks. They were buried deep in the ground.

It was impossible.

And yet, here it was: the most powerful phantom he had ever encountered. It had no place on this earth. It was alien in this time, and Donald had no idea what to do.

He could hear Merry's thoughts: *Will it eat me?*

"I don't *think* it can eat us," whispered Donald. "But it might crush us."

"This is one wild hurricane," remarked Danny. "I feel like Dorothy in *The Wizard of Oz*."

Through a storm of fear, Donald saw the creature's body and forearms were coated in small dark feathers.

"Can't you see it?" asked Merry incredulously.

"See what?"

"Shh." Merry grabbed Danny's arm. "It might hear you."

"You're bananas," said Danny fondly. "Storms have got eyes, but they don't have ears."

The dinosaur cocked its hideous head and stamped round. Its nostrils widened as big as dustbin lids. "What's it doing?" Merry crouched lower.

"Sniffing," whispered Donald.

"Why's it angry?" Merry tried to make herself smaller.

"Because it's a giant flesh-eating dead dinosaur. Does it need a reason?"

"It looks like a *Tyrannosaurus rex*, but with feathers," said Merry.

"No one has ever seen a *Tyrannosaurus rex*," whispered Donald. "We don't know that they didn't have feathers."

"Why are we hiding?" complained Danny, standing. "I'm wet."

"Shhhh." Merry and Donald dragged him down.

But the dinosaur had heard them and swung round in their direction.

"Should we run?" Merry's voice was shaking.

"We can't outrun it," said Donald quietly, his heart banging.

The dinosaur took a step closer. Then it roared. A blast of stagnant air smelling like rotten meat hit the children. A series of images flashed through Donald's mind.

Teeth. Fangs. Knives. Swords. Shark mouth. Razors. Knives. Lion. Biting. Jaws. Tongue.

Without warning, it rushed at them. The massive, three-toed feet thudded closer and closer. The children were knocked flat by a wave of impossible energy as it flew over them. Donald lay on his back. As he looked up, empty-lunged, the thick-skinned underside of a long, powerful tail passed overhead.

In one movement it was at the nest, stalking round and peering in.

"Am I alive?" whispered Merry.

"Who knows?" gasped Donald. He swallowed some air and felt a delicious rush of oxygen soothe his lungs.

"Can we run now?" Merry was watching the dinosaur with wide, frightened eyes.

"If you can," breathed Donald.

But Danny lay beside them, his eyes shut.

"Danny." Merry got to her knees and began shaking him. "Wake up."

He opened one eye. "I dreamed I was in the washing machine."

"Shhhh," said Donald. He slowly got to his knees. "Come on, Danny. Imagine Mrs Higgins is after you."

"What?"

"Time to get into the Safe Space," said Donald softly.

Danny sat up, his clothes drenched.

"But I haven't thumped anyone," he said in a dazed voice. "Have I?"

"I'll thump you if you don't get a move on," said Merry.

"He's concussed," said Donald. "He's not thinking straight."

"So what's new," said Merry darkly.

"Danny, we're at school, and we're skiving assembly," said Donald quietly but firmly. "We've got to creep past the staffroom window."

"I'm your man," murmured Danny. "Let's go."

The children crept away from the dinosaur.

As soon they were back under cover of the Christmas trees, they ran as hard as they could, putting as much distance between them and IT as they could.

"It's not coming after us," coughed Merry. Light-headed with relief, they stumbled and tripped down the path back to the caravan park.

Merry pointed at the horizon. "It's nearly morning." As a grey light crept over the distant hills, the world seemed to fall silent, apart from the pattering of the children's feet over the stones and mud.

Donald felt a small surge of energy.

"We'll beat it," he said. "We have to."

Back in the caravan, the children collapsed on the sofa. According to Donald's watch, it was five past one in the morning. But it most likely wasn't that time, because his watch had stopped two years ago. He still wore it because it had been his dad's. When Donald looked at his watch, he only knew what time it probably wasn't.

They could hear Mum snoring through the thin walls.

"Should we wake her?" Merry's clothes were splattered with mud and the hems of her trousers were soaked. She had a long scratch on her cheek.

"No a way," said Donald, also filthy.

Danny Olini lay on the sofa with his feet on the window. "You two," he said fondly. "Making up your ickle stories."

"Danny, there is a giant ghost dinosaur rampaging round Dorset," said Merry. "It has caused tens of thousands of pounds' worth of damage."

"You're kooky, but you're funny," yawned Danny.

"Oh shut up," said Merry. The caravan was cold, so she bent to light the gas fire.

Donald watched as a dark shadow slid through the tin wall, glided over the carpet and stopped at his feet.

"Wake up, Dozy Donald." Danny lightly slapped Donald's arm.

"Wait," said Merry. She recognized that look. "He's seeing something."

The weave in the sofa cushion turned into an ear; the table leg grew thick and covered in black hairs.

"Hello, Bear," said Donald, tickling his massive ears. The dog grinned and licked his paw.

Merry moved her feet from where Bear was sitting. "If Bear is back, that means one of us is in danger."

"Or all of us," said Donald. "Which is reasonable,

considering we are working out how to tackle a colossal prehistoric demon."

"How do you normally sort out ghost problems?" asked Merry. "What's your formula?"

Donald caught Bear's yellow eyes gazing steadily at him.

"I sort of chat to them," he said. "Most problems can be sorted out with a chat."

"Good luck chatting to a dinosaur," said Merry.

"Dinosaurs have small brains," said Donald. "They're just eating, sleeping, roaring machines."

"Like Danny," said Merry.

"Are you teasing me?" Danny sat up in delight. "If you are teasing me, it means you fancy me."

"No it does not," said Merry promptly.

"Ha," said Danny.

"Don't 'Ha' me." Merry blew her nose with her fingers. "I'm not being rude to you because I fancy you. I'm being rude because you're annoying."

"You'll change your mind. I'm growing into a very attractive man."

"Who told you that? Your blind grandmother?"

"No, the mirror told me," said Danny. "Don't worry, I can wait for you to come to your senses."

"You'll be waiting for a long time," muttered Merry.

"Love is eternal."

"Oh, please shut up," said Merry.

"Excuse me?" Donald waved. "I'm trying to sort out a deadly situation here."

"So am I," said Merry, scowling at Danny.

"Sorry, Donald," said Danny. "I can't help hitting on your bird."

"I AM NOT HIS BIRD," roared Merry, getting to her feet.

"We're friends," protested Donald. "Can't boys and girls be friends without everyone talking about it?"

"No," said Danny. He eyed the others. "One thing I am never sure of is, are you two actually 'going out'?"

"Oh leave off." Donald glanced at Merry and wondered if he wasn't just a tiny bit jealous of her bickering with Danny. Bickering with Merry was something HE liked to do.

Someone was banging on the caravan door. When nobody got out of bed, the banging was transferred to the front window. When still nobody got out of bed, the walls started to shake as someone thumped them. Donald put his pillow over his head and waited as he heard his mother's bed creak and the door open.

He heard low voices. He took the pillow off his head.

"*A . . . what?*" he heard Mum say.

Very carefully, Donald got out of bed and stood by the door.

"*No!*"

Whisper, whisper, whisper.

It was Estella's voice. Donald hadn't seen her since the swimming pool disaster.

WHISPER.

"*I don't know if he knows. He might. You know what he's like.*"

Donald did not like being talked about when he was not there. Even if he was there, which he was.

"Hi," he said, pushing open his door.

"Darling." said Mum. She fastened her purple dressing gown more tightly around her. "We've had some news."

"We need your help," said Estella. She was wearing black trousers, a black woolly jumper. Her hair was swept back from her face with a black scarf and she was holding a plastic bag. She looked cross but excited.

Merry's door opened. Half of her hair stuck up like a beaten fan. The other half was twisted into a runaway plait. Not looking at anyone, she scurried past and settled herself at the table.

"What is that?" Estella pointed at a huddle of clothes on the sofa. "Is it a manifestation?"

"Sort of. It's Danny Olini," said Merry.

Estella hesitated. "This is information of a most sensitive nature," she said, her gaze flicking over Merry.

Danny chuckled in his sleep.

"He won't wake up," said Merry. "We're safe. He's in stage three of his dream cycle. Even our headmaster can't drag him out of that."

Estella sat as far from Danny as she could. "He has a disturbing aura."

"How can we help you?" asked Mum, trying to take control.

"I need you to meet someone." Estella got out her mobile

phone and tapped in a number. Everyone sat in awkward silence whilst it connected.

"Mr Townley. It's me. Can you come right away? It's caravan number five six seven nine."

Mum sucked in her breath. It wasn't very polite to invite strangers into other people's caravans.

But Estella wasn't bothered about annoying Mum. She placed something on the table.

"Know what this is?"

It was a shiny grey rock about the size of Merry's fist.

"It's a shiny grey rock, about the size of my fist," said Merry.

"It is a bezoar," said Estella, rolling the *R* sound.

"What's that?" asked Merry.

"A coprolite," said Estella, wrinkling her nose.

"Is that a fossil?" asked Donald. It made him see mustard and fog.

"I thought every schoolchild knew what a coprolite was," said Estella.

"Not these ones," said Merry under her hand.

"Dinosaur excrement," said Estella.

Donald picked up the pebble. "This is dinosaur poo?" It didn't look like poo. It just looked like a rock, and rather a pretty one at that.

"Poor dinosaur," muttered Merry. "Imagine pushing and pushing. . ."

"Stop," said Estella. "There is no need to be crude."

"Poo is crude," said Donald. "It's poo."

"I'd have thought dinosaurs would have done bigger

182

poos than that," mused Merry, taking it from Donald and weighing it in her hand. "I'd have thought they would have had dumps as big as footballs."

"Depends on the size of the dinosaur," said Donald wisely. "This one can't have been that big."

Estella clapped her hands. "Thank you, children, for that illuminating discussion. May I continue?"

Merry hurriedly put the coprolite on the table, where it chattered to a standstill.

"The thing that is causing all this disturbance is. . ." She paused, her eyes sweeping the little room dramatically. "The spirit of a prehistoric monster. A terrible, unthinking lizard."

"No," breathed Mum, so surprised her glasses fell off her nose.

"Yes," said Estella. "I have seen evidence of the soul of a dinosaur." Estella turned her gaze on the children and looked penetratingly at Donald. "Have you seen anything like this?"

Donald shifted in his seat. But as he was about to speak, he saw something out of the corner of his eye and got a jolt like an electric shock. The shadow of a spirit was waving wildly outside the window. It was so faint, it was like a reflection in water.

Donald couldn't say a word.

Because it was Dad.

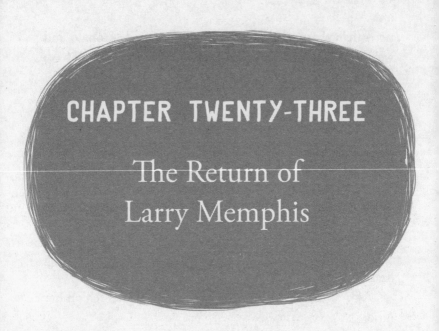

CHAPTER TWENTY-THREE

The Return of
Larry Memphis

"Dad?"

Dad mouthed "NO" and waved his arms like he was treading water. Donald clamped his hand over his mouth.

"What's that?" Estella twisted her long neck to look out of the window, just as Dad faded into the metal frame of the neighbouring caravan.

"Um, Dad would have loved this. He was crazy about dinosaurs," fumbled Donald.

"He was?" said Mum.

Merry gave him a quizzical look. Very gently, so no one else would notice, Donald shook his head. *Don't ask me anything.* Merry sometimes seemed to read his mind. Maybe she could do it now.

"Why are you shaking your head?" asked Estella.

"He's got an ear problem," supplied Merry.

"He has?" Mum looked alarmed.

Donald still couldn't speak. Dad! Here! Dad, who rarely left his house, turning up seventy miles from home. What could it mean? Donald wanted to charge outside and find him right away.

Estella cleared her throat. "We believe a dinosaur spirit has been unearthed by the recent landslides." She gauged everyone's reactions. "We must find its bones and put it to rest before it does terrible harm."

Merry suppressed a yawn.

"This is not surprising news to you?" asked Estella suspiciously.

"Most very surprising," answered Merry quickly.

"Donald, we will need you." Estella turned to him. "As you are a supremely gifted child, we will need all your skill."

Donald nodded and nonchalantly glanced out of the window, hoping to catch another glimpse of Dad. Under the table, Bear licked his hand.

"Does that dog have to be in here?" asked Estella suddenly. "Dogs make me itch. Even dead ones."

Mum looked dismayed. "Oh no, is Bear back, Donald?"

Donald knew he ought to be alarmed. But he liked having Bear around, even if it did mean he was in deadly peril.

There was a gentle knock on the door.

"Come in," commanded Estella as if it was her caravan. Donald watched Mum bristle.

The door opened and a man in his twenties with tousled blond hair and a red coat entered.

"This is Wilf Townley," said Estella, standing. "And his assistant, Claire Voyant."

The young girl medium put her head round the door and gave Donald the unfriendliest smile he'd ever seen.

So much for saving her life.

"Hi, guys!" said Wilf brightly. "Great to be here! Crazy stuff! Sorry I'm late." He smelled of ironing. He reminded Donald of the moon, he had such a shining firm face. Then he remembered. Wilf Townley was the celebrity palae-on-tol-a-thingy. He'd seen the poster in the café in Lyme Regis.

Claire Voyant was talking to Mum. "I'm a spiritualist, but my day job is assistant to Mr Townley."

Donald felt himself going red. He'd thought Claire Voyant was only fourteen or so.

"Goodness! You look so young," gushed Mum, pulling out a couple of stools.

The caravan felt very small and crowded.

Actually, the caravan WAS very small and crowded.

"This is all pretty wild, hippie magic stuff," beamed Wilf. "But I'll play along." He stroked a shark tooth hanging round his neck. "So you want me to go fossil hunting?"

"We do," said Estella firmly. "We need you to find the bones of the creature that has been causing all this trouble. Some of us have actually seen it." She looked very hard at Donald. "And we know it is a large carnivorous dinosaur."

"We know more than that," said Claire, surprising everyone.

(She even surprised me, and I am writing this blooming story.)

"I saw it at the swimming pool before I fainted. I drew a picture and showed it to Wilf. He thinks he knows what sort it might be."

Wilf took off his red coat, revealing his snow-white T-shirt and smooth TV-presenter arms. "I usually do my identification from fossils, not drawings. But it could be a *Megalosaurus*. A big meat-eater that lived in the UK. It fits the description."

Wilf went on. The dinosaurs lived in small family groups and built nests on the ground (here Merry raised an eyebrow at Donald). They fed off small animals and smaller dinosaurs. They became extinct around one hundred and sixty million years ago.

"It must be really, really angry," said Merry. "How come all the other dug up fossils don't behave like this?"

"You guys," smiled Wilf. "I kind of believe the ghost thing, but also don't believe it one little bit, you know?'

"So what now?" asked Mum nervously. "We know what it is, or was. How do we stop it?"

Estella leaned back against the wall. "We need to join forces." Again she looked at Donald. "We need Wilf to find the bones, and we need Donald to keep watching for any sign of the spirit."

"Why me?" asked Donald.

"Because you're the best in the land," said Estella simply.

Donald felt himself glow with pleasure. The BEST IN THE LAND!

Claire Voyant glared at him. "Have you seen it?"

"Sort of," faltered Donald. "No and yes. Maybe but maybe not. I felt it, but it wasn't there, y'know?"

"The best in the land?" said Claire Voyant suspiciously.

"I'm not having Donald go out on a crumbling cliff face," said Mum quickly. "It's too dangerous."

Estella fixed her gaze on the light fitting in the ceiling. "The fabled maternal instinct rears its inconvenient head. Don't worry, April. We will keep him quite safe."

Under the table, Bear let out a tiny growl, so quiet only Donald could hear it.

"Well, I'm game," said Wilf, leaping to his feet. "This is the craziest job I ever did, but I'm a player, you know?"

"We're paying him a fortune," whispered Claire Voyant. "Celebrity fossil hunters don't come cheap."

Mum cleared her throat. "I have two things to say." She spoke in rather a shrill voice which manifested itself when she was upset. "Firstly, I am coming too. And secondly, Donald isn't going anywhere without having had breakfast. And he needs a shower. So if you wouldn't all mind leaving, we will meet you in the car park in one hour."

"Oh for goodness' sake," said Estella. "All right. But speed is of the essence. Who knows when it will come back."

Wilf offered his hand to Donald to high five. "Looking forward to working with you, buddy."

They slapped palms.

Wilf's hand reminded Donald of park benches and river grit.

"Let's see how talented you really are," sneered Claire Voyant, stalking out.

When everyone had left, Mum locked the door.

"I'm not happy about this. It's no job for a child. What does Estella think will happen when you find the bones? The spirit will come and thank you and sleep for eternity? You can't bargain with a force like this. I'm going to take you both home."

"Mum," said Donald, still half dazed. "I saw Dad."

Mum swivelled very slowly to face her son. "Are you sure?"

"He was outside the window when Estella was here."

"Don't tell Estella," said Mum. She put the cornflakes on the table, missed, and the flakes went all over the floor, like a dump truck emptying a load of rubble.

"I think you must have imagined it, or saw a spirit that LOOKED like Dad. He doesn't leave his house."

"But, Mum. . ."

"I said. . ." Mum froze.

The cornflakes on the floor had started to rise in the air, one by one. They hovered around Mum's knees, then swirled round in a spiral up to the ceiling. The bin lid opened and they plummeted in.

Donald blinked and there was Dad, a little fainter than usual but very much him, sitting at the table and holding out his arms.

"Dad!" Donald ran to hug him. He felt cold and had a strange charge about him, like he was full of static electricity.

"Is that is what you call a dramatic entrance?" asked

Merry, trying to sound cooler than she felt. For she could see him too.

Mum backed to the wall. "How did you get here?"

"Hello, April," said Dad. "You look well."

"You don't," she said shortly.

"I see you're driving a taxi. Has The Charmer finally died?"

"It's like you," said Mum. "It keeps coming back to life."

"I haven't got much time." Dad sounded like he was speaking in the next room, though he was right there. "I have a message from the Otherworld. There's danger here."

"But, Dad, how *did* you get here?"

Dad sat on the table. "It wasn't easy. And I'll be pulled back to Bristol soon. But you need to stop them."

"Stop who?"

"The Witch," Dad said, glancing at Mum. "The Witch and her servants. Your mother knows who I mean."

Mum snorted. "I wish you wouldn't call my friends witches. Anyway, we're not stopping anything. We're going home."

"Estella's your *friend* now?" said Dad incredulously. "Watch her. She's deadly. She'll stop at nothing to get what she wants."

Mum clattered cutlery in the sink in an annoyed fashion.

Dad took Donald's hand. "Listen. I know what you are dealing with. The dinosaur. But there's something else. Estella has got hold of something very dangerous. I don't know exactly what or why. But there are terrifying ripples in the Otherworld! I've been sent here by powerful spirits."

"What is the Otherworld?" Merry whispered to Donald.

"It's where all the Nothings are when they're not here," replied Donald.

"And what powerful spirits have sent your dad here?"

"Dunno," said Donald. "I didn't know ghosts had bosses and things."

Merry tsked.

Dad turned to Mum. "April, I need you to take Donald to High Cliff. I'm told there is someone there he needs to meet. Someone who will help. Don't trust Estella. Please." He was beginning to fade.

"I ought to take them both home to Bristol," said Mum, beginning to waver.

"Estella must be stopped." Dad was now more not here than here.

"Where are you going?" Donald grasped at the air where Dad almost was.

"All right," said Mum grudgingly, "but we're not staying for. . ."

But Dad was

gone.

191

CHAPTER TWENTY-FOUR

The Dragon Hunter

Leaving Danny sleeping (Mum called Mrs Olini and told her where he was), they scuttled into the Dazzle Van and drove out of the caravan park by the back road, keeping an anxious eye out for Estella and her friends.

"Why does Dad call Estella 'The Witch'?" asked Donald.

Mum sighed. "He doesn't like her. And she doesn't like him."

Donald had guessed that already. "Did *she* kill him?"

"Nooooooooooo," squeaked Mum. She sighed. "They used to be engaged, years ago, when he was still alive. But he left her for me."

"Eeek! That's gross!" said Donald. "So why doesn't she hate you too?"

"Why should she? I didn't leave her, did I?"

"But why did Dad warn me about her?"

"Estella is a very powerful medium," Mum said, steering on to the main road. "Lots of ghosts are wary of her."

"Because. . .?" prompted Merry.

Mum gripped the steering wheel very tightly. "Because even before she knew your dad, she used to be a vicar."

"So?"

"So she has all sorts of ways of dealing with ghosts. And anyway, when your father was alive, he didn't even believe in ghosts. He just thought I had a wild imagination." She sighed again. "He thought Estella was filling my head with nonsense. He wanted me to give up my medium work.'

"*Dad* didn't believe in ghosts?" Donald was incredulous.

"How ironic," said Merry.

"Is that why you divorced?" asked Donald.

"A tiny bit. There were other boring reasons." And that was all Mum would say.

Look, just so you know, I'm NOT going to go into all the boring reasons why Donald's parents got divorced. You don't need to know the ins and outs of everything, do you? Don't be so blummin' nosy! Focus on the story!

They were driving along the coast road with the sea spread out below them. It looked cold and unfriendly and made Donald think of margarine.

"Let's have an ice cream when we get there," said Mum in a false-bright voice.

"No one eats ice cream in February," said Donald, still feeling margariney.

"I do," said Merry, hopefully.

The Dazzle Van stopped in the clifftop car park. The police tape had been replaced with a plastic fence. There were signs dotted along the edge.

DANGER, CLIFF FALL

"Let's make a plan," said Mum. "We are NOT going to be bullied by anyone, dead or alive."

"I'm just going to get some fresh air," said Merry. "Back in a mo." She opened the door and stepped down. She was feeling strange and left out. What use would she be against the phantom dinosaur?

The wind blew in her face and up her sleeves as she trudged along the cliff path.

This was definitely the oddest holiday ever. She thought of her large family and her cat, Sampson, and felt a twinge of homesickness. She watched a ship on the horizon and imagined herself standing on the deck, leaning against the railings and looking back at England.

Someone tapped her on the shoulder.

"Hello, dearie."

Merry jumped. Standing there, wearing a long dress belonging to another century, a bonnet and a wide smile, was a very real ghost.

"Hello," said Merry uncertainly. The woman was in her late forties and had black grey-streaked hair. Her face was pink and she had weather lines over her forehead and cheeks. She smelled of wind, mud and sweat.

194

"I heard you wanted to go seeking curios?" said the woman. She spoke with such a funny accent Merry wasn't quite sure she had heard correctly.

"I guess." Merry knew "curios" was the old-fashioned word for fossils. She checked behind her to see if Donald had spotted the ghost. But he was still in the Dazzle Van with his mum.

"My name is Mary Anning," said the ghost. "I know a bit about fossils and the finding of them. I can help you."

Mary Anning. The name was familiar. Merry gasped. "You're Mary Anning! You're famous! We learned about you in school. You found a sea dragon! I mean a plesiosaur." Merry remembered it all now. Mary Anning had found many famous specimens and was a real expert.

Mary Anning had gone pink along her hair line. "Well now," she said. "You've heard of me! Well, well. There you go." She turned to look at the sea, still muttering to herself. She seemed very pleased.

"I'm Merry Al-Haroud." Merry held out her hand.

"Mary! Like me!" Mary Anning had such rough skin on her fingers it was like shaking hands with a scouring pad.

"No, Merry as in happy," explained Merry. "My parents chose kooky names for their kids."

This was amazing. Mary Anning was the first celebrity Merry had ever met. (Wilf didn't count because she's never heard of him before this week.) OK, Mary was dead, but it was still impressive.

"I'm told some bones have been moved and the spirit has risen," said Mary Anning. "I hear it could be a type of land dinosaur. So odd. It should be a sea creature in these cliffs."

"I've seen it," said Merry. "It looked a bit like a *Tyrannosaurus rex*, but it had feathers. Wilf Townley said it was a megalosaurus."

"How unusual," mused Mary Anning. She whistled. "Let's get on." A little dog bounded over from nowhere. He was a black-and-white terrier with a bald scar on his head. He had one brown eye and one green. His tail wagged furiously as he sniffed Merry's boots.

"Tray!" said Merry. "We read about him. But didn't he. . ." She stopped. Mary Anning's dog was killed in a cliff slide. Did the ghost Mary know about this?

Mary pointed out over the cliff. "We need to be down there on the beach," she said. "There's a path but it's hard to find. You'll have to follow me." She took Merry's elbow. "Mind you go careful and look out for the others."

"The others?" asked Merry. "What others?"

"Those fossil thieves," said Mary darkly. "Ever since a big landslide last month, we've had a team of strangers plundering the coast with their axes and dynamite, stealing the ancient bones and then who knows what!"

"Do you mean the tourists?" asked Merry, feeling rather guilty. She had taken a fossil or two from various beaches before.

"No, dear, not the families and trippers. There's a

woman. A woman with The Sight. I stay out of her way. She's no friend to spirits."

"Is she tall with brown curly hair and a posh voice?" Merry wondered if she was talking about Estella.

"She is." Mary Anning marched off over the grass, her dog running at her skirts.

"Come along!" she called over her shoulder.

"Er, hang on." Merry waved at Donald and April, who had appeared on the path behind her.

"Who's that?" Donald called rather rudely, Merry thought.

"Mary Anning, the fossil hunter. She's going to help us find the dinosaur," explained Merry as he puffed over.

Donald's face brightened. "Oh, she must be the one we're supposed to meet. She's famous, isn't she?"

"Yes, but she's not like, starry," said Merry.

Mum looked wildly round. All she could see was the cliff edge, the sea and the sky.

"I don't see anyone!" she wailed.

"She's a GHOST," Donald couldn't help snapping.

"Oh," said Mum unhappily. "I'll follow you, then."

"Come along, Miss Happy!" called Mary.

"Miss Happy? You?" Donald's eyes bulged with amusement.

"Shut it." Merry nudged him. As they ran to catch up she took Donald's arm.

"Do ghosts have an address book? How did she know to find us?"

"I don't know. I'm not dead," said Donald.

The path cut deeply into the cliff and as the children climbed, they saw layers and layers of rock, laid down over the years.

"It's like going back in time," said Merry, running her finger over a smooth orange layer. Various plants and mosses grew out of the stones, and peering into a crevasse, Donald saw a very old bird's nest with a tiny ghost worm inside.

Mary was waiting for them at a bend in the path.

"Where are your tools?"

"We haven't got any," said Merry. "This is Donald, by the way, and April, his mum."

"I'm pleased to make your acquaintance," smiled Mary. "Can your mother see me?" For Mum was looking very hard at a space where Mary wasn't.

Donald fired a ? at Mum.

"I detect a presence," breathed Mum happily.

"Hallelujah," said Donald. Bear slunk up and he rubbed the dog's head.

The little group rounded a sharp corner and the beach spread out below them. A small crowd of people stood perilously close to the overhanging cliff.

"Stay low," said Donald. "Don't let them see us."

A woman held a television camera on her shoulder and a man in a yellow jacket wrestled with a long sound boom. They were recording a man with blond hair who was showing something to the camera.

"That's Wilf Townley, the celebrity fossil hunter," said Merry. "He's supposed to be waiting with Estella for us at Belle View car park."

"What's he doing?" asked Mum as Wilf put an object into his mouth and bit it.

"He's having his lunch," said Donald, who, as well as the gifts of first, second, third, fourth and fifth sight, also had jet-fighter-perfect eyesight. "That looks like a cold burger with lettuce and tomato relish."

Everyone felt hungry.

"I've never found anything of those, what did you call it? A *megalosaurus* along this stretch," said Mary Anning. "This used to be a sea. Not land. I only find sea creatures. But it doesn't mean it isn't here. Maybe the creature fell in."

Merry brightened. "Imagine a massive megalosaurus being chased along the clifftop by another gigantic dinosaur, wanting to bite its head off. . ." She bared her teeth as she went through the actions, playing the parts of both dinosaurs. "It stumbles . . ." Merry dropped to her knees. ". . . and falls hundreds of feet into the boiling sea. Then its flesh is devoured by Mary Anning's sea dragons and its bones settle on the ocean floor, where it is gradually covered by silt and over hundreds of thousands of years it becomes fossilized."

"The land shifts, the oceans move and the seabed becomes a cliff," said Donald.

"No wonder it's cross," said Merry. "If it was just about to eat its dinner when it died."

Donald shook his head. He'd liked the story up to this part. "No, this spirit is angry about something, but it's not hunger."

Merry and Mum swapped a look. Donald had his super-sense face on.

Mary Anning tapped her stick impatiently. "We need to get along. The tide will be up in the hour." She bolted down the path, her skirts flapping round her ankles.

As they got closer, Donald recognized more people.

Estella Grey was wearing a long black coat and keeping well away from the television camera. Close to her stood Claire Voyant and Old Joe.

"Don't let them see us," said Donald.

"I don't see why," said Mum. "We're all on the same side. We all want to find and stop this great beast. I think your dad was just overreacting." A gust of wind blew her hair over her face and into her mouth.

"Estella is a bit creepy," said Merry. "Sorry if that's rude."

"Of course she's creepy." Mum spat out hair. "She's the central medium for the south-west. She's a chief witch and a gold-badge magic woman. You can't be all those things without being a bit creepy."

Donald sniffed. He could do all the things Estella could and more, and HE wasn't creepy. At least, he hoped he wasn't.

"Dad said we shouldn't trust Estella, remember? We're supposed to be staying away from her."

Mum hesitated. "Darling, when you get divorced, you HOPE your ex isn't still going to tell you what to do. And when your ex dies, you should doubly be free of their orders."

"But this is Dad," said Donald, growing warm. "He might be your ex-husband, but he's not my ex-dad."

"Do hurry," called Mary Anning.

Mum patted his shoulder. "Don't worry, if we meet Estella we won't say anything."

Slipping on rocks and clambering over boulders, they all reached the bottom. The beach was a mixture of sand, pebbles and large outcrops, and the sea was a good distance away. Estella and her group were now round the corner and out of sight.

"Don't go close to the cliff," said Mary. "They slide and fall without warning."

Donald looked at the towering mass of stone above them. He felt his mind sharpen and focus, as he listened for rhythms of the long-dead. He heard a gentle humming and low vibrations, but nothing he could communicate with.

"Not here. Let's look further along."

Mary looked at Donald with respect. "You have the eye," she said. "I never even found an ammonite on this belt of cliff. It is sterile."

They walked for ten minutes in the opposite direction to the other group. Mary Anning never lifted her eyes above the ground, searching every dark hole and inspecting every pockmarked rock. Every so often someone would find something to show Mary and she would nod and politely tell them that no, it wasn't a fossil, but was a very pretty stone.

"What are we looking for?" asked Merry after about ten minutes.

"Patterns," Mary Anning replied. "The curve of an eye socket. The knobs of a vertebrae. The point of a tooth. When you see one, the rest become clear."

It was a bit like seeing ghosts, reflected Donald. You hear a noise here, see a sparkle there, smell something where it shouldn't be.

Mary Anning led them round the base of a landslide, where a heap of rock had come away from the cliff and lay smashed on the beach. "Look here." She had a stick which she used to turn over the stones. Merry and Donald watched as she picked stones up, turned them over, and split them apart with her hand axe.

Then Mary Anning picked up some more stones, turned them over, threw them away, or split them apart.

Then Mary Anning picked up some rocks and threw them away.

Then Mary Anning found a stone, split it in half, and threw the bits away.

Then Mary Anning. . . OK, got it? This is what Mary Anning did for about half an hour before Merry folded her arms and said: "This is SO tedious."

"We're trying to save the West Country from the ravages of a demon beast and you are bored?" said Donald, who was also bored, but didn't want to admit it.

"What's wrong, Miss Happy?" asked Mary Anning. "This is fun! Out in the weather and wind, searching for treasure."

"We're modern kids," said Merry. "We're used to being entertained by screens, pressing buttons in the warm, building universes and destroying alien spaceships."

"But you can build universes with these remains," said Mary Anning, her eyes shining. "I find fantastical beasts that were real!"

"It's harder work than our fun," admitted Merry.

"How about a quick break? There's a café back there," said Donald hopefully. He thought longingly of a baked potato slathered in butter and cheese. The mist slaked down the crumbling cliff and crept under his collar. His hair curled in the dampness. Then he saw something further down the beach which made him flinch and forget all about his lunch. Something that was walking towards them on the edge of the foaming surf.

"What's up, Donald? You're a bit freaky-looking," said Merry. "No offence to you as his mother." She nodded at Mum.

"None taken," said Mum. "Sometimes I think he looks a bit freaky too."

"Look," said Donald.

Estella Grey was walking up the beach. "Enchanted that you're here. We spotted your car," she called. "Such a distinctive colour."

Behind her was Wilf Townley and his TV crew.

And behind them were Claire Voyant and Old Joe.

And barely there, shrinking and blending with the rocks and the sand, staying out of everyone's vision except for Donald's, was Larry Memphis.

CHAPTER TWENTY-FIVE

The Curio of Curios

Estella Grey was pretending not to watch Donald.

The ghost of Mary Anning was pretending not to watch Wilf Townley.

Wilf Townley was pretending not to watch himself.

Merry wasn't not-watching anyone, but she was fascinated by the ghost of Mary Anning and kept finding herself not-watching her.

You can watch whoever the heck you like.

Everyone was searching along the same belt of rocks. Estella's cronies were working the hardest, smashing stones and swarming over the landslide.

Donald could sense Dad on the very edge of his

consciousness, like a vague thought you'd had three weeks ago. And Bear stuck to his heels so closely Donald could feel his cold breath.

"Who is that?" snapped Estella, finally noticing Mary Anning. "Can you go away, please? We're on serious fossil hunting business here."

"Oh, I'm a nobody," said Mary. "I was a nobody when I was alive and now I'm dead I'm definitely nobody. Don't let yourselves get too close to the cliff. People always forget." She turned back to the rock.

"Hello, hello," said Wilf, inspecting a wide flat rock. "What's this?"

Mary Anning took a quick look. She tsked and drifted back to her original spot.

"False alarm," said Wilf. "It's a smear of mud."

"Don't entertain us, just do your job," said Estella crisply.

Wilf looked bashful. "But it's my job to entertain when I'm being filmed. I'm supposed to keep up a running commentary."

"Don't bother," said Estella. "You're not on television now."

"It's tricky to stop thinking I'm being watched by millions of people," smiled Wilf, flicking his hair. "I'm used to having my every move screened all over the world."

"Forget them," said Estella. "No one is thinking about you right now."

"Oh," said Wilf, crestfallen. "Someone somewhere might be thinking about me. I have a big Facebook following."

"No," said Estella. "Most people would choose cheese

on toast over a meeting with a low-level television presenter."

"Righty ho," said Wilf humbly and went back to work. Donald felt sorry for him, though it was true, he would choose cheese on toast too.

"So can you do it?" Estella asked Donald. "We need to find the creature as soon as possible."

Mum coughed a warning kind of cough.

Donald shut his eyes, mainly to avoid the hot-metal scrutiny of Estella.

He could feel the ghost of a large lost whale, out in the sea beyond the rocks. He could also clearly see the spirit of a backpacker, standing very close to the edge of the overhanging cliff. There were a couple of cheerful ghost dogs bounding in and out of the surf, but there was no sign, no whisper of IT. The ghosts of the ancient sea dragons and dinosaurs had long faded. Or maybe there was something. He felt a pinprick of dread, and a strange feeling that spread up from the soles of his feet to the top of his scalp.

"Feel something?" asked Estella sharply. "Where should we dig?" Even Claire Voyant looked up with interest.

But then it was gone. Donald's stomach rumbled. An image of melting cheese came to him. He was hungry, that was all.

"It's nothing," he said.

Mum smiled at him.

It's all right. I'm here. We can leave whenever you want.

Her thoughts came to him as clear as anything. He had read his mother's mind.

"We can go home whenever you want," she said.

"I know," said Donald. He was always good at guessing what people were thinking.

He shot a furtive look at Estella and gasped as he felt something like a slap in the side of his jaw.

No. You can't read my mind, young man.

He hurriedly turned away.

He felt a light, almost not-there, tap on his arm.

The ghost of Mary Anning smiled shyly. "Look where the Blue Lias is layered below the clay and limestone? That layer is over one hundred and ninety million years old. It's where I find most of my Jurassic curios. I found the sea dragon there all those years ago." Mary directed him to a mound of rock which she said had recently fallen from the cliff above.

Donald felt the tiniest hint of something dark and ancient. In his mind's eye he saw an oval shape, pulsing with a golden spark inside. He looked down and his eyes were drawn to a patch of shale not far from the cliff. It seemed to jump with sparks and he heard the echo of an ancient cry of something large and reptilian.

"Over there?" Mary Anning had followed his gaze. So had Wilf Townley. And so had Estella. In an instant, all three were picking at the rock, Mary frowning as the others pushed in front of her.

"It is supposed to be a gentlemanly sport."

"Quiet, spirit," roared Estella. "We must find this demon's bones."

"I think I can see something unusual," said Mary, poking her rusty old hammer in a hole.

"There's something unusual in here," said Wilf, his voice rising in excitement.

"I saw it first," said Mary.

"It's very exciting to be the first one to discover a new fossil," said Wilf.

"It might be nothing," said Mary.

"It might be nothing," said Wilf.

Donald wondered who was reading whose mind. Wilf and Mary had kind of swirled into one mad celebrity fossil hunter mass.

"AHA," they both shouted. "WHAT'S THIS?"

"A marvel," said Mary, hacking away a large lump of rock.

"Awesome." Wilf knocked off a big chunk.

"What is it?" Donald and Estella asked together.

Mary peeled off a large scoop of clay and gasped as a long length of bone came into view.

"Oh my cockles," she said in delight. "Oh my alive alive O!"

"It's the shin bone of a biped," said Wilf excitedly. He whipped out his phone and handed it to Donald. "Quick, film me uncovering more."

"But if I film you, I won't be watching in real life," protested Donald.

As they watched, Wilf and Mary revealed more and more bone – first the remains of a ribcage, then a taloned foot.

"It's huge," said Merry. "Is it IT?"

Estella looked at him sharply. "Donald?"

Donald saw in the fossilized bones the ghost of the great

beast they had seen a few nights before, stalking the cliffs and bellowing in fury.

"Yes," he said.

Fifteen minutes later and the tide was creeping closer. There was only a narrow strip of beach left.

Donald was surprised how much he was enjoying himself. Now there was something to do, he got absorbed in scraping the layers of mud to reveal more bones, like uncovering a mosaic. Merry too was muddy, but happily working on the tail.

Before them lay the fossilized remains of a vast dinosaur, some ten metres long, with feet as big as sledges. Long back bones led to a curved, frightening, alien-looking neck, the vertebrae gleaming against the stones and mud. The skull, with dead eye sockets and a jaw full of ferocious teeth, looked like something out of a nightmare. The remains were flattened, frightening and very dead.

The sky darkened around the little group as thick, wet-looking clouds rolled over the sky. A chilling wind blew in from the sea.

"We need to leave," said Mum, watching the sea.

"Why has a land dinosaur been found in an ancient seabed?" mused Wilf Townley. Oblivious to the tide, he had started digging again.

"All the supernatural powers in the world cannot save us from the sea," said Mum.

"Quiet," snapped Estella. "Wilf has found something else."

Mary and Wilf were fighting for space in a spot near the dinosaur's tail.

"WOW!" shrieked Wilf. "The WORLD should see this."

"It is worth returning from the grave for this," smiled Mary, not seeming to mind that Wilf was standing in her foot.

Donald saw them immediately. A cluster of seven oval objects in a depression beneath the dinosaur's foot. Each was about the size of his shoe.

"Eggs," said Donald and Merry together.

"Eggs," said Mary and Wilf.

"Eggs," said Estella and Claire.

"This must mean our dinosaur is a girl," said Merry.

"One is missing," said Mary Anning. "Look at the indentation."

"It looks like one egg is missing," said Wilf Townley. He scraped at a pocket in the rock.

"Fancy that!" said Estella.

Mum coughed. "The tide is nearly in. Donald and Merry, you HAVE to come with me. Right. Now."

"But this is amazing!" said Donald. "This is EVERYTHING." He knew at once it was not the ghost of the megalosaurus he had sensed but the little vibrations from the eggs themselves.

"We can see them tomorrow," said Mum firmly.

"You sound very firm," said Merry.

"I am," said Mum. "Mostly."

"Go," said Estella, her eyes shining. "We will be along

later. We must at least save these precious eggs from the tides."

The ghost of Mary Anning stopped chiselling and looked at the waves.

"Hello again, Lady Sea," she said to the water. She whistled for her dog. "The eggs will keep. Tide only gets this high on the neap. But you will be cut off if you stay any longer." She collected her tools, waved at the children and vanished into the cliff.

"Mum, we can't go now. It's finally got exciting," protested Donald.

Bear padded up to Donald, looked at him with his misty yellow eyes and growled. The noise came from the depths of his stomach.

"All right," said Donald, because he didn't want Bear growling at him again.

"We'll look after these," said Estella. She touched Donald's shoulder with her long chilled fingers. "Thank you for showing us the way."

Then Donald and Merry had to leave, Mum hurrying them along the sand and pebbles over the narrow strip, back up the cliff path to the Dazzle Van.

Donald wearily climbed into his seat. His legs ached and his hands were caked with dirt. His boots had leaked and his feet were wet. But what a find! The heater was blasting out hot air and he kicked off his boots, pulled off his wet socks and wriggled his damp, wrinkled toes.

The empty seat next to him was no longer empty. A very blurry and faded Dad sat next to him, his finger over his almost transparent lips. Donald stared. His dad looked like a ghost, a normal one, instead of the warm, solid-ghost Dad he knew. It was horrible.

"Did Mary Anning help you find the eggs?" he whispered, so quietly the only other occupant of the car that heard him was Bear.

Donald stared. How did Dad know about the eggs?

He nodded.

"Good. Do you have them safe?"

"Still on the beach," Donald mouthed. "Estella is with them."

Dad closed his shadowy eyes.

"Is that bad?" asked Donald, forgetting to be quiet. "We had no choice . . . the tide. . ."

"Is what bad?" asked Merry from the front. She turned round. "Oh, hi, Larry."

The van skidded to a stop as Mum slammed on the brakes.

"What?" she said, pulling over on to the side of the road. She unclipped her seatbelt and stood in the well between the two front seats. "Larry? Why can't I see you? Where is he?"

But Dad had gone.

"Was he really here?" demanded Mum. "What did he say about the dinosaur?"

Donald shook his head. "He wasn't here for long," he said. "I got nothing."

As they rattled back to the caravan site, Donald looked at the darkening countryside. Would the dinosaur go wild again tonight? How could they work out what was annoying her? Then he heard a very faint whisper, as quiet as one of his own thoughts.

"*Estella has taken the eggs. You must get them back. She means to do great harm.*"

"What sort of Great Harm?" asked Donald.

"*Nobody knows.*"

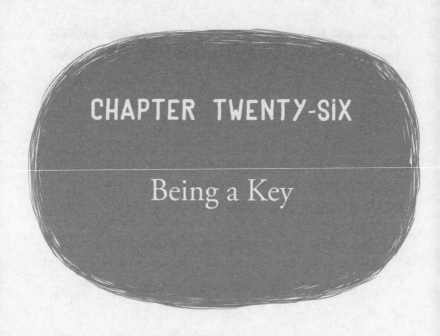

CHAPTER TWENTY-SIX

Being a Key

"Home tomorrow," sang Mum, bundling up dirty washing.

"We can't go home," said Donald, biting into his melted cheese on toast with extra pickle. "We've just found the bones. And the eggs! Dad says Estella will do Great Harm."

Mum dumped the dirty washing next to the TV. "He always was a drama queen. Now you've helped Estella locate the bones, I'm sure she can deal with this troublesome ghost. It's not a job for a child or me. Now, who would like to watch a film tonight?"

Donald would never have described the mighty and powerful dinosaur as a "troublesome ghost", like IT was some naughty spirit who liked stealing pens.

"Do you want *Star Wars*?" asked Mum. She was, Donald thought, being DELIBERATELY DISTRACTING.

"Where are Estella and the others staying?" persisted Donald. He hadn't sensed her presence in the holiday park.

"There's a mystic fayre being held in a castle near here. Estella's group have hired some barns attached to the castle. They're all there."

"What is it called?" asked Merry.

"Castle Drum," said Mum. "It's got such pretty gardens and real cannons on the terraces and the girls were telling me they do this wonderful lemon cake. . ."

"Let's go tomorrow," said Donald.

Mum looked at her son suspiciously. "You want to go to a mystic fayre?"

"Uh-huh." Donald nodded. "Me and Merry can look around the castle and you can visit the fayre."

Mum clapped her hands together. "That sounds perfect! There is a seminar on recognizing Ectoplasm which I would simply LOVE to attend. . ." She stopped. "This is to do with IT, isn't it? You've played your part, leading the experts to the bones. Now you must let them lay IT to rest. I don't want you getting into trouble."

"How can we get into trouble in a garden?" asked Donald innocently. "Who's that for?"

Merry was writing a postcard. "Sampson," she replied.

"But he's a cat."

"So? Mum will read it out to him."

"Why don't you just send him a text message?"

215

Merry scowled. "Don't be thick, Donald. Cats don't have phones."

During *Star Wars*, Mum fell asleep. The gas fire was on full blast and the room was full of a damp fumey heat. Donald paced the worn carpet. He could only take four steps before he had to turn and come back, so it wasn't very satisfactory pacing.

"Dad said we have to get the eggs back."

TAP TAP TAP

"Dad, is that you?"

Donald went to the window. A broad face with heavy features and a wide smile grimaced at him through the glass. Danny Olini.

Donald reluctantly let him in, wondering if there would ever be a time when Danny Olini turned up and it wasn't an unpleasant shock.

"Don't wake Mum," he ordered as Danny bounced in.

"News, guys, news!" said Danny. He opened the fridge and took out a peach yoghurt. He ripped off the lid and squeezed the contents into his mouth. "Gross," he said.

Ignoring the sleeping Mum, he sat on the flimsy table. "My mother dragged me to some boring castle, yeah? I sneaked off to the café and I met that Wilf Townley, the TV guy, eating lemon cake. Anyway, I fooled him I was freaky like you, yeah? Don?"

"How could you be like me?" interrupted Donald, half flattered, half disturbed.

Danny grinned. "I told him I had magic powers. I

thought I might get on the telly. I went off with him to the witches' HQ in these big sheds and Wilf was talking about fossils and dinosaurs and I pretended to see a ghost! Funny! I said I saw an old-fashioned chick in a red dress. Wilf believed me. Funny!" Danny did a star jump from the table and landed on his knees.

"Hi, Merry," said Danny. "Whatcha watchin'?"

"*Star Wars*," said Merry.

Everyone watched the TV for a few minutes. Then Donald gently said, "Danny, you have news for us?"

"Yes, yes," said Danny, tearing his eyes from the screen. "Wilf Townley thought I was in the inner circle of witches. He's dumb, isn't he?"

"Mediums," said Donald. "They're not witches, they're mediums."

"That's arguable," remarked Merry.

"Wilf took me in this room in the barn FULL of fossils. There were big ones, little ones. Said he thought it would help me if I knew what I was looking for. And then I saw these eggs in a padded black box. They were dinosaur eggs! Seven of them! Wilf said you'd helped find them."

Donald paced faster. He looked at his mother. Mum was sleeping snugly under a red fluffy blanket, her face a picture of calm. Did she know anything about this?

"Then that tall woman, Estella, came in and saw me with Wilf in the barn. She was like, 'Who is THAT BOY?' and Wilf was like, 'ER?' and I said, 'I'm Danny Olini'. And Estella said, 'THIS ROOM IS PRIVATE', and 'WHAT HAS HE SEEN?' and Wilf gave me a look look, you know?

I liked old Wilf, he brought me a ham wrap and juice and was a funny guy and I didn't want to get him into trouble, so I said, 'Nothing but some old stones', and everyone went, 'Phew'. At least they would have if the whole thing had been a comic."

Donald and Merry gave each other a meaningful look.

Danny Olini watched them. "I KNEW you'd be interested. I'm the detective round here. I found the metal sculpture, and I found the eggs. So tell me, what's it all about?"

"Ghosts," said Donald. "Nothings. Spooks and spirits."

"Funny guy," said Danny. "If I didn't like you, I'd bash you."

"You like me?" Donald was touched.

"Course I like you," said Danny. "I don't hit you, do I?"

"Not much."

"There you go," said Danny. "I'm going to see if I can get on the roof of our caravan. Want to come?"

"No," replied Donald.

"Never mind." Danny got up. "Imagine everyone's faces when I dangle upside down in the window." He bounced to his feet and took a flying leap across the kitchen and out the door.

Merry waited until she was sure he had gone before she spoke.

"Do you think the dinosaur is going to be even more annoyed now *all* her eggs have been removed?"

"Yes," said Donald.

"So what are we going to do?"

Donald switched off the TV. "I'm hoping my dad is going to help us with that."

Where was Dad?

He looked up. "I'm fed up with you," he said quietly. "Always following me around and making little comments."

"Me?" said Merry, shocked.

"Not you, Merry. YOU."

He looked into the void. But everyone knows there is nothing in voids. Only Nothing.

"Are you talking to a ghost?" asked Merry, bemused.

"Sort of." Donald glowered. "YOU KNOW WHO YOU ARE."

Silence.

"I can't see any ghosts," said Merry. "I still need more practice."

"It's a Nothing, but it's not a DEAD Nothing," said Donald. "It's something that is watching me The Whole Time. Reading my thoughts, discussing me. Talking about US. It's like an annoying shadow, yip, yip, yipping in my ear and trying to be funny."

Hang on.

"Yes," said Donald quickly. "YOU."

YOU!

Eeeeek!!!

"Yes," said Donald. "I can sense you too, you know."

Eeeek eeek!

Does he mean . . . me?

"Yes, you," said Donald. "You're confusing me. I'm trying to work out what to do and you keep making stupid jokes."

But I'm the narrator. I'm telling your story.

"I don't know what you mean," said Donald. "But keep it down, OK? You're putting me off. You make me think of almonds."

He's broken through! He can sense us! You and me. Especially me. This never happens. Donald is really Very Talented.

"Shut up," said Donald.

"This must be a very odd Nothing," said Merry, warily.

"It is," said Donald.

Umm. Right.

Goodnight.

"Goodnight," said Donald sternly.

Almonds!!!!

It is a universal law that if it has been raining a lot on holiday, it will be sunny on the day you go home. Therefore, when Merry* opened her eyes on Saturday morning, she saw a band of gold peeping round her orange curtains. She heard gulls screeching and the far-off wash of the sea.

The shower switched on with a thump and the calm was broken by the whine of the hot water pump. Donald's mum broke into song. "OH WHAT A BEAUTIFUL MOR–NING, OH WHAT A BEAUTIFUL DAY."

---

* You may have noticed I am talking about Merry, not Donald. That is because I'm a bit freaked out by him at the moment. Don't worry. I will get back to him soon. Just give me time. OK?

Merry crawled out of bed and walked the two paces into the kitchen, where Donald was contemplating the fridge.

"Have you heard from your dad?" asked Merry.

"Not yet," said Donald, pouring milk on his cornflakes. "But he said we have to get the eggs back off Estella. So we go to the Castle Boombox, or whatever it is called, ditch Mum, then somehow get into these barns and find the eggs, steal them back and then. . ."

"And then what?" asked Merry.

"Dunno. Wait and see what Dad says," said Donald.

"Let's hope he turns up," said Merry darkly. She watched Donald eat.

"You went a bit strange last night, talking to a Nothing."

"Sorry," said Donald. "Sometimes I get fed up with the Nothings. Sometimes I wish I could just turn them all off."

*

Nothing is happening here because Donald actually managed to turn off his extrasensory perception and blocked off everything. Including us.

*

OK, we're back. Let's go.

Castle Drum was a vast brown stone building with four square towers.

Vast by Donald's standards, anyway.

There was a dodgy rainbow sign on the gate that said "Mystic Fayre".

"How fabulous," breathed Mum. "I might get some new crystals."

By eleven o'clock, she was safely tucked away at her session entitled "Recognizing Ectoplasm". and Donald and Merry had five pounds each to entertain themselves. They wandered into the central hall of the castle, a lofty oak-panelled space with a stone floor and an enormous fireplace. There were witches, mediums, fortune tellers and spiritualists. Lining the room were stalls selling pots of coloured charms and tins of incense. Packs of tarot cards were laid out in circles and wind chimes and bell ropes jingled and tinkled. There were witchy clothes: cloaks and long velvet dresses hung in colourful lines. There were books on magic, spell kits and paintings of goddesses. Colourful scarves floated from hooks and jewel-coloured candles wafted sweet scents. There was a tent where you could go and get healed by colours, and another where you could get healed by light. The boom of drums from a sound bath echoed up into the arched roof.

Merry nudged Donald. Red, green and blue Sardonique sisters were standing in a sunny alcove, taking part in a chanting workshop led by a woman with brown hair down to her ankles. The children noticed more people they'd rescued from the Belle View swimming pool milling about.

"Is this place haunted?" asked Merry.

"If it is, they'll be scared off by this lot."

"Donald Memphis!"

Donald and Merry gaped as the Reverend Hattie Bisto

bore down on them. She was wearing a purple dress and a green headscarf dotted with tiny dragons.

"I'm enchanted to see you again!" She glanced from side to side. "May we converse? Let's peruse the gardens."

Donald was dumbfounded. Surely vicars weren't supposed to like all this witchy, spiritual stuff?

"I adore all of this," smiled Hattie. "So good to keep abreast of all spiritual activities."

Outside, they crossed a wide wet lawn, surrounded by daffodils, primroses, snowdrops and crocus. They passed under a stone arch and crunched over gravel to a bench by a stone lion.

As soon as they were settled, Hattie began to talk.

"I will try to speak plain. I've been trying to get hold of you but to no avail. You won't know this, but Estella Grey is an old acquaintance of mine."

Donald leapt up. "What?"

Hattie took his elbow and gently guided him back. "Please be seated. I am actually an undercover spiritual investigator, and I am currently investigating Estella. You also won't know that last month, an ancient dinosaur egg was found on the beach. It was deposited in Lyme Regis Museum. It was stolen the same night." Hattie smoothed out her dress. "I believe Estella stole it."

Donald's mind was whirring. He remembered the indentation in the rock next to the other seven eggs and Mary Anning saying one was missing.

"I think the missing egg is key to this large psychic disturbance, the wild weather, the crazy storms."

"It's a bit far-fetched," said Merry.

"My whole life is far-fetched," said Donald. He frowned at Hattie. "What has this got to do with me?"

"Because of who you are and because of this." Hattie reached into the folds of her dress and brought out her phone. "Estella sent one of my spies this text last month." She tapped a few buttons and showed them the screen.

"I'm not The Key!" shivered Donald. "I like to keep low-key, not be The Key. And if this was sent last month then. . ."

Hattie smiled. "Yes, I knew you were special before I even met you at the church."

Donald felt a bit freaked out. "But you called Mum to

settle the Dead Rev – I mean, the Reverend Frank Bird."

"Oh, him." Hattie waved her hand dismissively. "I've put up with him for years. No, I asked your mum to come so I could find out more about *you*."

"Eeek," said Merry.

Hattie looked at the time. "I must go. Can we talk later? But for now, I must ask you to keep out of Estella's way. She's staying over there." Hattie pointed to some low barns behind the main building. "Don't go anywhere near her." She stood, looking like a giant plum.

"Take Especially Great Care." Patting Donald's head, she whipped off over the grass back to the castle.

Merry stretched. "She doesn't talk like a spelling test any more. I suppose this means we can't go and nick the eggs, if you're The Key."

"I don't want to be The Key," said Donald, resting his chin on his knees.

"Well, I can't be The Key," said Merry.

"Why not?" asked Donald. "You'd make a great Key."

"This is a pointless conversation," said Merry.

"It's better than trying to break into a building and stealing some demon dinosaur eggs from a creepy witch woman," said Donald. "But that's what Dad wants us to do."

"Hattie said to stay away!" protested Merry.

"She might be a double spy," retorted Donald. "She might secretly be Estella's bestie."

"Hide," Merry grabbed Donald's wrist and dragged him behind a large clipped bush, as Estella herself came out of a wooden door in the side of the nearest barn. They watched through the leaves as Estella, followed by Claire Voyant and Old Joe, crossed the lawn.

Merry felt herself relax as Estella reached the main door, then froze as she deftly turned and stared in their direction.

"She hasn't got X-ray vision," whispered Donald.

But Merry couldn't breathe until the three had vanished into the castle.

"Right, then," said Donald. "Let's go and collect some eggs."

CHAPTER TWENTY-SEVEN

Eggs

The barn smelled like hot cheese. The floor was made of shiny rectangular stone slabs and the very clean windows were tall and arched. The children stood in a wide hallway with numerous doors. It was a dead kind of place, with no ghosts, no spiders or bugs and no trespassing slugs. There was no dust and the too-white walls were spotless. Donald passed a dark painting and noticed his reflection. His hair looked like he had been fighting wild men.

He cautiously tried the handle of the nearest door. It was locked. At door number thirteen, Donald stopped.

"There's someone in there," he mouthed. "But it's like they're asleep, but not asleep."

Merry felt tingles of alarm run up her arms.

Bravely, Donald knocked on the door. "Hello?"

Then Merry heard it too, a tiny shift in the silence, like a lazy cat thinking.

"Can't you unlock it using your special talents?" asked Merry.

Donald frowned. "I'm not a magician."

He tried the door, and to his astonishment it opened.

"Yes you are!" said Merry.

"It was already open," protested Donald.

The room had bunk beds on one side, and a table and chair on the other. The curtains were drawn and when Merry went to pull them back, she tripped on something.

"UMM UMM," said the something and Merry yelped. There was a large foot that was wagging, in a white trainer, attached to a leg. "Umm umm," it said again.

Merry whipped away the cloth.

Wilf Townley sat on the floor, his hands strapped behind him and a green handkerchief tied over his mouth.

Merry took a step back. Was this some kind of crazy TV thing? She removed the gag.

"Yuck. It wasn't even clean!" spat Wilf.

"That's gross," said Merry.

"I must look dreadful," said Wilf. "Do you have a mirror?"

"No," said Merry.

She and Donald worked at the knots behind Wilf's back whilst he gabbled.

"It was Estella and Old Joe! I found out what they were

228

up to, and when I threatened to expose them on national television, they tied me up! Thank goodness you kids came along." He screwed up his face. "I've got excruciating pins and needles."

Finally untied, Wilf gave a weak smile. "I guess I'm a real celebrity, now there's been a kidnap attempt."

Donald went out into the corridor to check nobody was coming and when he returned, Wilf was doing stretching exercises.

"So what is Estella up to?" Donald asked.

"I'll show you." Wilf pulled a suitcase from under the bed. Inside was a Tupperware box, a hammer and six dinosaur eggs.

"We got caught by the tide but Estella wouldn't leave without them. We had to leave the megalosaurus or we would have drowned. We had to climb the cliff as it was." Wilf passed an egg to Donald, who cupped it in both hands. It was smooth and yellowish, and very heavy. Donald felt his teeth go on edge, like he was chewing tinfoil.

"Cool, huh?" said Wilf, handing an egg to Merry. "It's over one hundred and sixty million years old."

"It feels weird," said Merry, promptly giving it back. "I don't like thinking there's a tiny dead dinosaur inside."

Wilf put the egg back in the suitcase and brought out the Tupperware tub.

"This is just astonishing," he said. He wiped his eye. "I can't believe they did this." He opened the lid. Inside was a kind of grey, powdery sand.

"What is it?" asked Merry.

"I called in on Estella last night. I was crazy with excitement about the eggs. I had an idea for a TV show about me and the dinosaur, so I came here, to Castle Drum. I thought they would be chuffed to see me! I am a celebrity, after all." Wilf swallowed. "I walked in on them smashing up one of the eggs with a hammer!"

"No!" Donald was jolted.

"I could have been an investigative journalist. . ." said Wilf.

"Wilf, focus! Why was Estella breaking up the egg?" persisted Merry.

"As soon as they saw me, they jumped on me and tied me up! I've only been to the loo once in twelve hours! They fed me this horrible tea from a machine and a cheese sandwich. I don't eat bread. It bloats me."

"WILF," Merry said sharply. "Stop talking about yourself and tell us more."

Wilf tugged and patted his hair. "At first I thought they were cooking. They had water and some plants and bits and pieces, and a little cooking pot here in this very room! But then – oh, you won't believe me."

"Try us," said Merry.

"They put the egg powder in the pot!"

"Prehistoric omelette?" asked Merry.

"I know what they were doing," said Donald quietly. "They were making a spell."

"What kind of spell would need ground-up dinosaur eggs?" asked Merry.

"A powerful one," said Donald. "Merry, find Mum

and tell her what's happening. Me and Wilf will take the eggs, try and find Hattie and meet you back at the Dazzle Van."

"I'm gone," said Merry, slipping out of the room.

Donald touched the dinosaur powder. All that history, crushed into nothing. How sad. He saw a volcano and thick clouds of ash.

"C'mon, mate," said Wilf. "Those crazy witches could be back at any minute."

Donald sealed the lid of the box and rewrapped the remaining six eggs. He wondered if the eighth egg, the one that had been stolen from the museum, had been crushed up too. Was that why IT was so cross?

Then they crept out into the corridor. Sunlight shone through the very clean windows.

"Are we stealing them?" asked Donald. "Who do they belong to?"

"I found them," said Wilf. "They're mine."

"I don't think the dinosaur would agree," said Donald. "We need to get them back to her."

Wilf looked pained. "Mate, I really need the toilet. I've been tied up so long, I had to hold it in. But now I think it is coming out and. . ."

"I'll be outside," said Donald.

Wilf nodded and scuttled through a door with a loo sign on it. It was a ladies' loo but Donald assumed ladies' toilets worked as well as the men's.

But as he carried the box towards the exit, the door opened and a shadow slid over the floor.

231

Donald halted, horrified, as Estella glided towards him, flanked by Claire Voyant and Old Joe.

"Hello," she said in her smooth voice. "I wondered when you'd show up."

Her eyes fell on the box.

"You have something of mine."

CHAPTER TWENTY-EIGHT

Close to Nothing

Merry found Donald's mum browsing a stall full of crystals. The stones shone and sparkled in the light and cast rainbows over the walls.

"I thought you were supposed to be at a seminar on recognizing ectoplasm," panted Merry.

"I know." Mum smiled guiltily. "But everyone was so gloomy. I decided I'd rather come and look at rainbows than talk about dead people."

"But it's your job," said Merry, rather shocked.

"I'm on holiday."

Merry quickly explained what she and Donald had found.

"Wilf was tied up?" Mum glanced around to make sure no one was listening. "They did WHAT to the dinosaur eggs?"

"It was so mean to crush up those eggs. No wonder the dinosaur went mad. They might be the only kind left. It's like making them double extinct," said Merry furiously.

"You can't make something extinct twice," mused Mum. "You're either extinct or not. Anyway, I've found out something." She steered Merry through the stalls and out into the gardens.

"Estella is working on a very powerful spell," she whispered. "I was in the loo and I overheard the Sardonique Sisters talking. Estella has got a VERY big project. It's about. . ." She paused. "Tell me, do you see any ghosts?"

"No," said Merry.

"The spell is about getting rid of bad ghosts." Mum spoke in a low voice.

"How spooky," said Merry, shivering a little. She didn't like to think about bad ghosts. She looked at the bright garden flowers to reassure herself.

"Estella is making a spell to get rid of the really tricky ones. Like the dinosaur, I suppose." Mum spoke so softly Merry could barely hear her. "Because exorcism doesn't always work."

"Isn't it good to get rid of all the bad ghosts?" asked Merry.

Mum shook and nodded her head at the same time. "Who decides what ghost is good or bad?"

"Isn't it obvious?" asked Merry.

They had nearly arrived at the car park, but there was no Donald or Wilf.

"One person's bad ghost might be someone else's good ghost," explained Mum.

"Oh, let's not worry about that now, let's just find Donald," said Merry. But when they reached the Dazzle Van, Donald was not there.

Donald stood on a wide, flat stone, close to the edge of the cliff. The seabirds screeched overhead. Old Joe grasped his arm, forcing Donald close to his chest. Donald stared at Joe's necklace of suns, moons and tiny skulls, hanging close to Donald's nose. He had a hollowed-out feeling in his stomach. He didn't think he was going to be thrown off the cliff, because Bear was not here. And Bear knew if people were about to be thrown off cliffs. All the same, he couldn't help asking, in a small voice:

"Are you going to kill me?"

Estella's lips stretched into a smile and her tongue snake-flickered.

"That would be a waste. I hope not. I don't want to harm you and you'd make a formidable spirit." She took a heavy old book from her bag and started leafing through the pages.

Donald felt faint. He pulled away from Old Joe but the man only gripped him tighter, his fingers burrowing into Donald's flesh like his arm was made of plasticine.

He'd been bundled into the back of a car, with Old Joe holding him the whole way. He'd shouted and yelled but

Old Joe's strong hand clamped over his mouth in such a way that he couldn't bite it. Claire Voyant had driven out of the castle car park, and turned left down a green lane. It was very bumpy and the car's wheels had stuck and spun all the way.

Donald had thought briefly about crying, then decided he was too angry. How DARE these people kidnap him like this? They were supposed to be his mother's sort-of friends.

"What do you want with me?" asked Donald.

Estella sighed, a sigh which ended in a little growl. "My dear, talented Donald, I need you." She turned to him. Her skin looked stretched to breaking point over her skull. "There's a ghost we need to destroy. A greedy, unnatural spirit who has taken up more than its fair share of this world. A ghost that acts like it is still alive!"

"This is about the dinosaur, right?" Donald felt fear churn his guts. "But you're the ones who called her up by stealing her egg from the museum and destroying it."

"There are many ways of settling problems." Estella smiled nastily. "Your mother likes to reason with the spirits. I prefer a more direct approach."

"You're going to exorcise the dinosaur," said Donald. "And you need me to help?"

Estella was silent.

Now the group stood close to a trig point, a stone marker, high on the cliff. A mountain of stone and rock and earth lay on the beach below where there had been a landslide. Estella and her gang had built a fire next to the trig point, and had laid a board on top, and on top of this were bowls

236

and cups of various contents. Donald could also see the tub of dinosaur powder.

They were remaking the spell.

Donald shifted uneasily. "You're not going to grind me up, I hope," he said in a small voice.

Estella smiled. "You're much too valuable for that." She came closer. "It is going to LOOK like Old Joe is going to drop you off the cliff, but he isn't. He's just going to . . . to . . . dangle you. We need to lure something here, something that will only come if you are in very great danger."

"You might be double bluffing and throw me off anyway," stammered Donald.

"Noooooooo," said Estella. "Believe me, we celebrate LIFE, not death."

A cold thought entered Donald's brain. "You're not after Bear, are you?"

"What Bear?" Estella frowned.

That was a no, then.

She showed him a page in her book. The paper was yellow with age. "This is a very old spell book I came across quite by chance. It turns out to have exactly what I need." She laughed to herself.

Donald tried to read, but the writing was all scribbly and old-fashioned and the spelling was even worse than his.

Crushe ye bones ands egges of ye anciente demones to dust to conjure ye beastes do appeare and laye waste to the lande and alle spirites who roam abroade

"So you called up the dinosaur on purpose?"

Estella smiled and snatched the book away.

Claire Voyant dropped some herbs in the saucepan.

"Shouldn't that be a cauldron?" asked Donald, wincing as Old Joe tied his hands behind his back with a scarf.

"Mine leaked," said Claire.

"Are you sure you lot aren't witches?" asked Donald. He half expected someone to produce a broomstick. He pushed off Old Joe and wriggled his fingers to get the blood back.

Estella shrugged. "We do not define ourselves by a job description."

"Mum does," said Donald. "She calls herself a Ghost Liaison Officer."

"April Memphis doesn't use a tenth of her powers," scoffed Estella. "She's more concerned with mothering –" Estella spat out the word "– than using her supernatural gifts."

"Really?" Donald was shocked.

"The spell is nearly finished," announced Claire Voyant. "The time has come. Lure forth the demon ghost."

Donald did not like the sound of this.

"To finish this spell, we need a very strong ingredient, the strongest in the world," said Estella in a strange high-pitched voice.

"What's that?" asked Donald nervously.

"To lay down ALL SPIRITS WHO ROAM, we also need the strongest human power – the power of love!" cried Estella.

Old Joe nudged Donald closer to the cliff edge. The rocks below looked hard and deadly.

238

Then, with a shot of pure terror, Donald saw Bear bounding up the cliff path at great speed.

Not Good.

All at once he felt a very strong presence and he gulped in relief as Dad appeared right next to him.

"Dad," said Donald. "They're going to hurt Bear, or me!"

Dad ruffled Donald's hair. "It's all right, Donald. It's not the dog they want, or you. It's me."

CHAPTER TWENTY-NINE

How to Kill a Ghost

Merry and Mum flew up and down the hallway of the barn, trying all the doors.

"Where are they?" moaned Mum.

"Can't you use your medium powers and call up Larry? He might know something?" Merry peeped under a crack of a door.

"Larry won't come anywhere near this place this weekend," called Mum, opening cupboards in the fossil room. "This is secret, but lots of mediums REALLY don't like him."

"Donald's dad?" Merry's mouth fell open. "But he's lovely!"

"He's unusual, for a ghost," said Mum, looking behind the curtains. "You can touch him, he's warm, he appears almost alive. Some mediums say, 'What if ALL ghosts were like him? The dead would hardly be dead'."

Merry swallowed. "But only Larry is like that. . ."

"As far as we know," said Mum darkly. "Estella has said that it might be best for humanity if ghosts like Larry had their spirits erased."

Merry gaped as she remembered something. "But YOU didn't like him when he was alive! You got divorced!"

"We got divorced because we didn't love each other any more," said Mum sheepishly. "To be honest, we didn't even like each other."

"But that's no reason to want his spirit erased," said Merry. "Or his life?" she added.

Mum looked thoughtful. "Well. . ."

"Is it?" demanded Merry. The conversation was taking a disturbing turn.

"Of course not," said Mum.

"And you'd protect his ghost for Donald?"

Mum looked amazed. "That's what I've been doing all these years. I've prevented the sale of his house, kept all the other mediums away, magnified his spirit with mirrors and charms. Most of my money goes on keeping that ghost alive, so to speak. It's quite generous for an ex-wife!" She swallowed. "Don't tell Donald all this, will you?"

There was the sound of a toilet flushing and running

water and they watched, bemused, as Wilf Townley came out of the ladies' loo.

"I feel better now," he smiled. "Where's little D?"

"He's with YOU," howled Merry, looking in the loo and hurriedly shutting the door again.

"He's gone to find you," replied Wilf.

Merry turned to Donald's mum. "Come on, Mrs Memphis. You're psychic. You MUST know where he is."

Donald's mum shook her head. "I'm out of practice."

"Do it!"

April sat cross-legged on the floor. She removed her glasses, put her hands on her chest and focused on a speck of nothing.

"OK," she said. "Here goes."

"Let him go," urged Dad. "Estella, please. You've lost your mind. How could you put the boy in danger? Get him away from the cliff."

Estella gazed at him with cold eyes. "The boy will be safe once you drink this." She held up a flask of shimmering, sparkling liquid.

The spell.

Donald was suddenly more frightened than he'd been in his whole life.

Everything Estella had been saying clicked into place.

A greedy, unnatural spirit who has taken up more than its fair share of this world. A ghost that acts like it is still alive!

"But this is my dad!" said Donald. Old Joe tightened his grip on his shoulder and edged him even closer to the drop. Donald looked down at the rocks far below. He felt his knees wobble and his ears pounded.

Estella drew herself up. "No ghost should walk the earth pretending he still lives!" she stated fiercely. "No ghost should be SOLID."

"I'm not *that* solid," protested Dad. "A little chubby, perhaps."

"You have a smell," said Estella. "Ghosts shouldn't smell that strongly."

Dad sniffed his armpits sheepishly.

"Larry Memphis is an ABOMINATION. Imagine if all spirits were like him. The dead would take over the world. There would be no room for the living!"

"Oh come on!" protested Dad. "I know you don't like me but. . ."

"You pick things up; you can PUT RECORDS ON," said Estella, growing wilder and wilder.

"Dreadful music too," said Old Joe.

"HE DOES NOT HAVE DREADFUL MUSIC," howled Donald.

"Thanks, son," said Dad. "Estella, I'm here. Please let Donald go. The cliff could crumble. . ."

"DRINK, THEN," said Estella.

"NO, you can't kill my dad!" screamed Donald.

"He's already dead," said Estella. Her eyes gleamed. "And you're the one who killed him the first time."

"What?" said Donald.

"That was mean," piped up Claire Voyant. "You didn't have to tell the kid that."

"Shut up," said Estella. "I'm making it easier for him."

"Estella, please. . ." Dad had squeezed himself on the narrow ledge between Donald and the drop.

As ever, he wore his black-and-white rugby shirt and his grey jeans. His stubble was nearly a beard.

"Did I kill you?" Donald stammered. "Is that why you and Mum never talk about it?"

Dad shook his head sadly. "It was an accident, darling. Not your fault."

"Yes it was," said Estella meanly. "You were a baby. You crawled out into the road. Larry ran to save you, and got knocked over by a lorry."

Donald felt a great sadness wash over him and for a moment or two, he couldn't speak. Everything made sense now. This was the reason his mum and dad wouldn't talk about Larry's death.

Donald swallowed, feeling the tears cluster behind his eyes. "Sorry, Dad."

Dad shook his head. "It was my fault. I should have shut the door."

"I never imagined it was anything like this." Donald stared at the ghost of his dad.

"We didn't want you to blame yourself," said Dad, smiling gently.

"The time has come for Larry Memphis to depart this earth," interrupted Estella. "And thanks to you, Donald, we can finish the job you began years ago. We knew your father would come to rescue you. So drink, spirit." Estella held out the bubbling flask. "Drink and then SLEEP."

"No!" shouted Donald, fighting to get free.

Ignoring Old Joe, Dad flung his arms around Donald. "It will be all right. Just stay away from too much disco. Rock music is a wiser choice."

"Don't drink it, Dad," said Donald, "or I won't see you again."

"Darling, they'll hound us for the rest of your days if I don't. It's true, I am an unusual ghost."

"Unusual is usual for me," said Donald, trembling and fighting to hold back the tears.

Just then, a human missile shot out from behind a gorse bush and rolled into the clearing. Danny Olini jumped up and kicked Old Joe hard in the leg, which made him topple over. At the same time he dragged Donald away from the cliff edge.

"Wow, thanks," said Donald.

"Where is she?" Danny roared at Estella.

"Who?" asked Estella. "You are an annoying child."

"I'm not here to rescue you, Donnie. Where's Merry?"

"Somewhere else," said Donald.

"Oh," said Danny, crestfallen. They looked back as Old Joe, rubbing his shin, charged after them.

"I'll be off again, then."

"You can't unrescue me," said Donald, looking wildly round for Dad as Estella tried to head him off.

Danny looked apologetic. "Well, really I came to rescue Merry." He paused. "Look at her!"

Claire Voyant had begun to sway like a tree in a hurricane. "We must call forth the demon. It is time."

"Drink the potion, Larry Memphis," shouted Estella, lunging for Donald. "Or we'll throw both boys off the cliff." Donald skipped out of her way, straight into the arms of Old Joe.

Claire Voyant raised the potion in her hands and began chanting.

"COME MIGHTY MASS OF ANCIENT LIZARD, TAKE BACK WITH YOU THIS FREAKISH SPIRIT."

"Don't call up the dinosaur," said Donald, trying to beat himself free. "She'll flatten us." He felt a surge of anger. "I saved your life in the swimming pool, Claire Voyant, some thanks this is!"

The wind began to blow harder.

"Oh no," said Donald, as a hum filled the air.

Claire Voyant wavered, but carried on chanting as the air grew dark.

"DRINK," screamed Estella, holding the potion to Dad's face.

Donald's mind was racing, trying to work out the connection between the potion and the dinosaur. It was clear Estella was trying to exorcize Dad, but this seemed a peculiar way to go about it. Estella was gripped in a trance. Her curls flew out wildly round her face and her long gown flapped in the wind.

"She won't stop now," said Old Joe, gripping him tighter. "She's waited years for this moment. Your dad is the hardest spirit she's ever tried to get rid of. He's the stickiest ghost we've ever known. Normal exorcism doesn't touch him."

Donald gaped. "You mean you've tried before?"

"Oh yes," said Joe. "Estella has tried to extinguish him many times. But she's got a new weapon now."

Dad was still trying to reason with Estella.

Donald remembered the time he had visited Dad and he saw a woman lurking outside, and how Dad had seemed like he was fading. Estella must have tried to do it then.

A wild hope rose in Donald's chest. If Estella, the most powerful medium in the country could not exorcize his dad, who could?

"The channelling begins," said Old Joe in his deep voice.

The clouds raced through the sky and the cliff grass was blown flat by a weird, blustery wind. As Donald watched, the sea shuddered and the waves began to turn and crash backwards. A clatter of pebbles rose from the beach, and spiralled up and up until they were swirling above the trig point. A fish spirit swam in the air, joined by another and another. A porpoise ghost shot out of the sea and swam through the air into the swirl. Next a ghost wearing raggedy trousers rose from the rocks and flailed through the air, followed by ghost seals, birds and rabbits.

It was as if a powerful magnet was drawing in every spirit around, just as had happened in the Belle View swimming pool a few days earlier. Donald watched a diver, clad in wetsuit and flippers, swim through the sky and join the supernatural cyclone.

Donald looked round for his dad, terrified he might join them.

"It's voluntary," called Dad. "All these ghosts want to go."

The ghost of Mary Anning sailed past, her long skirts billowing and flapping.

"Tis all right, dear, I've waited a long time for this!" she called. "Remember, don't get so close to the edge", and she was swept up in the flurry of noise and shapes and pebbles.

Donald took a quiet step back.

And another.

But strong fingers curled round his neck like a giant centipede had him in her pinchers.

Estella shoved him back to the cliff edge.

"DRINK, FOUL DEMON," she howled at Dad. "DRINK NOW. SHE IS COMING."

Donald's mind was racing, his heart hammering in his chest. Why was this potion so important? What made it work?

An image came to him, of a mighty dinosaur roaring in outrage.

Cold terror made his knees go weak and he stumbled.

"That's right," said Estella, watching him. "I can't extinguish Memphis, but something else can. The dinosaur cannot kill the living, but it will destroy a spirit who has eaten its eggs."

"A mother's wrath knows no end," said Old Joe, nastily.

Dad stood close to Donald and stroked his cheek. "Goodbye, darling. I'll always watch over you."

Then somehow the potion was in his hand and he held it to his mouth. A drop wavered from the lip.

"You're going to feed my dad to the dinosaur?" moaned Donald.

"She'll eat him dead or alive," sneered Estella.

Claire Voyant broke off chanting. "She's coming!" she shouted, her face suddenly filled with unexpected terror. "She's HERE."

"NO!" howled Donald. "No, no!"

A swirling fog blew up from the sea as a huge cracked and scaly reptilian talon clawed over the cliff, followed by a hideous malevolent head, the eyes boiling with malice.

CHAPTER THIRTY

The End

"Make it go away," cried Danny Olini, his face stiff with shock. "Donald. Help! It's looking at me!"

The enormous creature opened her jaws and roared and Danny Olini roared back in sheer terror.

Estella screeched with delight and for an instant Donald could see into her mind and read her thoughts.

She was picturing a boy tumbling off the cliff into the jaws of the beast.

"Me too?" he gasped.

"You're as much a freak as your father," yelled Estella.

"That's going too far, Estella," screamed Claire, unable to take her eyes off the monster. "No one said anything about hurting the boy."

The dinosaur's terrible eyes flickered and rotated until they were trained on Dad.

"Oh, Dad," said Donald. "Oh, Mum."

The Dazzle Van flew over the crest of the hill, beeping and flashing. Mum, Merry and Hattie Bisto came spilling out, followed by Wilf Townley holding a TV camera.

"How dare you kidnap my boy, you foul WITCH," screamed Mum.

In one movement, Donald elbowed Estella aside and leapt for the potion, knocking it out of Dad's hand and spilling it on the ground.

"Keep it rolling," shouted Wilf. "We're filming everything! Holy cow! What's that!"

He fell backwards as a mighty clawed foot stamped down on the cliff, shaking the ground. The fog cleared as the furious dinosaur bellowed and fumed, sounding like a thousand angry cats. She stood twenty feet tall and twice as long. Her long feathery tail lashed with displeasure. Her head darted to the ground and she eyed the box of eggs lying next to Estella. She let out an anguished roar and the ground trembled like a mighty train was passing beneath them.

"Run, Donald," bellowed Mum as the ground gave way and IT moved towards him. The earth opened up and pulled them both underground. The dinosaur ripped at the ground as it flipped over and caught Donald in a murderous knock, grind and rattle of boulders and a deadly pasting of wet soil. Sodden clumps of grass licked his face and fell away.

The cliff seemed to press Donald into its guts.

Am I going to be Nothing? thought Donald.

He didn't know how long he had been buried but his eyes were welded shut under layers of mud and stones. He couldn't feel his feet and his arms were pinioned to his sides. A thin plume of oxygen blew down a pinprick of light and he sniffed it in through his gobbed-up nostrils. Far below he sensed the dinosaur, but she was slipping deeper and deeper into the earth and then, with a sigh, like the last flickers of a fire, she and her eggs were gone.

WHAM! An intense pressure pulled at the back of his neck.

Donald had the sensation of being levered and plucked like a root from the soil.

Then he was lying out in the open. A freezing tongue licked his cheek and he opened his eyes to see Bear gazing at him, ivory front teeth bared in a dog smile and eyes twinkling with afterlife.

He was still alive, not Nothing.

Bear whined.

"Good boy," panted Donald. His voice sounded thick, like he had been swallowing custard.

Above him the mist had cleared to reveal a patch of blue sky, with a hint of sunlight.

He noticed a movement on the cliff and saw flashing blue lights. He watched Estella scramble up the side of the cliff into the six hands of three policemen. He saw the glint of handcuffs as they were snapped on her wrists.

Everything was still.

The next time he opened his eyes, there was a TV camera in his face and Wilf Townley was yabbering away.

"And now the remaining eggs lie buried under tonnes of rock. Who knows if they will ever see the light of day again? This is Wilf Townley, investigative reporter. . ."

Donald hadn't realized he'd been asleep, but he must have been because he was lying on the back seat of the Dazzle Van, his head in Mum's lap, with Merry squeezed in next to him.

The taxi was going very fast.

"You poor darling," said Mum. "I'm so sorry, I had no idea Estella was so wicked she'd use you as bait to get at Dad."

Donald rubbed his head, tried to sit up, then changed his mind.

"She wanted me gone too," he said in wonder.

"I thought she'd managed it for a while," said Merry, and squeezed his hand. "We saw you and the dinosaur go over the cliff. We thought you were a goner."

"Bear saved me," said Donald. He sat up. "Where is he?"

"We haven't seen him since we left," said Merry. "Which is good, because it means. . ."

"None of us are in danger," finished Donald. But he couldn't help feeling sad. What if he never saw him again?

Merry patted his arm. "Hey, this will cheer you up. All of Estella's crew have been arrested for robbery and kidnapping AND Hattie Bisto gave Danny Olini a lift back to the caravan park, and she was giving him a lecture on churches and you should have seen his face!" Merry chuckled.

"He sort of nearly saved me," said Donald. "Though he was really trying to save you."

Merry coughed. "So do you think the dinosaur has really gone now?"

"I think so," answered Mum. "She's been reunited with her eggs. She's buried deep."

"She's gone," said Donald. But as he spoke, a terrible thought sprung in his mind. He couldn't believe he hadn't thought it before.

"But Dad? Where is he? Did he drink any of the potion? Did he get eaten by the megalosaurus?"

Mum looked guilty.

"Mum? What happened?"

Then he heard a familiar voice.

"I'm here, darling. Who do you think is driving this thing?"

There at the wheel was Dad, his skin translucent, his stubble now quite definitely a beard, and a delighted smile on his face.

"You saved my life. I mean, my afterlife," said Dad. "Thank you, darling. I'm not quite ready to go yet. We've got lots more tunes to listen to."

He started humming a Bob tune.

So Donald settled back in his seat, happy that for now,

things were as they should be. And as the blurred hedges raced by, he quietly watched the huge dog shadow chasing alongside them.

iF YOU LiKED

HOW TO SPEAK SPOOK
(AND STAY ALIVE)

DON'T MiSS...

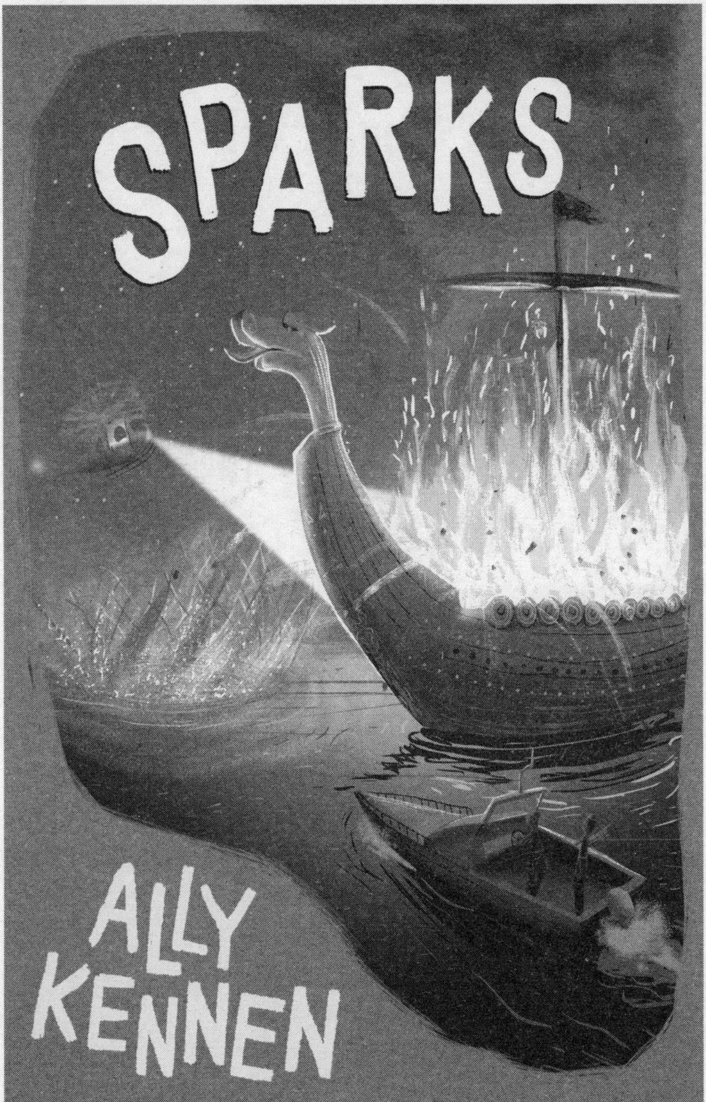
SPARKS
ALLY KENNEN

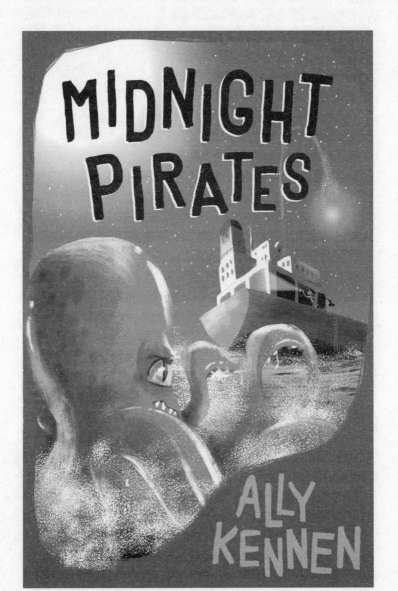